Lucas's lips had just ⬚⬚⬚⬚⬚ was a knock at her door.

They flew apart, both looking flustered and guilty.

"It's just me," a voice said.

Zoey sighed in relief. Benjamin, her older brother. She opened the door.

"I hope I'm not interrupting anything," he said.

"We were . . . uh, going over some homework," Zoey said lamely.

"Well, just in case, I thought I'd come up and warn you that Jake is downstairs in the family room."

"Jake?" Zoey cried.

"Yeah, you remember," Benjamin said, "your boyfriend? Big guy, muscles, dark hair? I didn't mention that you were up here playing tongue hockey with his worst enemy."

Lucas shook his head. "Maybe we should just get this out in the open."

"No!" Zoey said. "I mean, I want to prepare him for it."

Suddenly Benjamin froze, cocking his head to listen. "Damn. He's coming."

"Oh, no." Zoey looked pleadingly at Lucas. "Would you mind hiding? Quick?"

Jake's heavy tread was closer now, turning the corner at the top of the stairs. "Zo? Are you decent in there?"

Titles in the MAKING OUT series

And more fabulous MAKING OUT books
will follow!

MAKING OUT

Jake finds out

KATHERINE APPLEGATE

Pan Books

Cover Photography by Jutta Klee

First published 1994 by Harper Paperbacks

This Pan edition published 1995 by Macmillan Children's Books
a division of Macmillan Publishers Ltd
25 Eccleston Place London SW1W 9NF
and Basingstoke

Associated companies throughout the world

ISBN 0 330 34272 X

5 7 9 8 6 4

A CIP catalogue record for this book is available from
the British Library.

Printed and bound in Great Britain by
Mackays of Chatham PLC, Chatham, Kent

For Anne Brashares
and, as always, for Michael

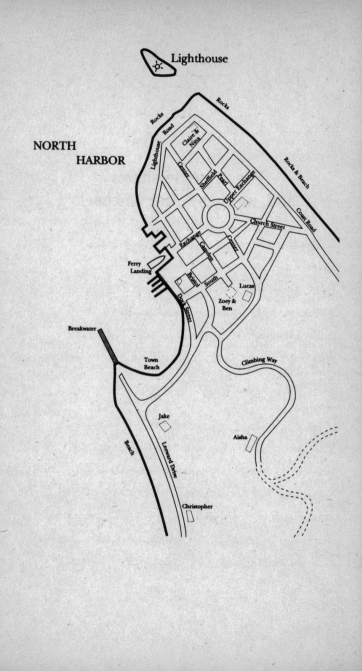

Zoey Passmore

Who is my boyfriend? Ha. Good question.

Truth is, I've sort of been torn between these two guys: Jake, my long-time boyfriend—a great guy, a nice guy, the right guy (according to all my friends)—and Lucas.

Lucas (according to all my friends) is the wrong guy. Very wrong.

See, a couple of years ago, Jake's brother, Wade, was killed in this car crash, and Lucas was driving the car. Lucas spent two years in jail for it. Then he got out, moved back here to Chatham Island, and, well, to make a long story short, I fell for him big time. Not _that_ big time, just, you know, kisses that stopped the moon in the sky and made my knees rattle.

I haven't told Jake yet. Maybe he won't care.

No, that's stupid. Of course he'll care. He loves me, he hates Lucas. The thought of me with Lucas will . . . I guess I don't know what it will do, except that it's bound to start trouble in our group. Living on a small island like this, it's very difficult to ignore how other people feel. And to show you just how popular Lucas Cabral is around here, his own father is planning to send him away. Mr. Cabral's very old-fashioned. He says Lucas brings shame on his family.

My friend Aisha thinks I'm being an idiot and that bad things will come from my being with Lucas. But I can't really believe that my loving Lucas could ever result in anything bad. I mean, it's love, right? And love conquers all. At least, I think it's love. Does probable love conquer all?

Probably.

Aisha Gray

Boyfriend? Don't start with me on the subject of boyfriends. There's this guy named Christopher who thinks he's my boyfriend. He thinks we're destined to become boyfriend and girlfriend because we're like the only two black kids on Chatham Island, if you don't count my little brother.

But I don't go for destiny. I don't go for fate. I am a rational person who is not going to be swayed just because some guy thinks he's hot, and everyone else I know thinks he's right for me. Zoey's the romantic in our group, which is why her life is a mess. I don't turn my life around just because some guy with a cute butt comes along.

Did I say that? What I meant was, I don't turn my life around just because some guy with a big mouth comes along. That's what I meant to say.

Anyway, if I wanted a boyfriend, there's a whole big world of opportunity: black, white, brown, yellow, red. I'm open-minded. And I make my own decisions. I'm my own woman.

So the answer is no, I don't have a boyfriend.

And if I did, it wouldn't be Christopher.

Nina Geiger

Don't have a boyfriend, never really wanted one. To me a guy is about as necessary as a training bra is to a python; as necessary as an inflamed appendix; as necessary as an electric blanket in hell.

See, that's my three-part comic tautology rule: If you're doing funny examples, do them in threes. Yes, tautology. Look it up. Use it in your next English class and watch your teacher fall over in a dead faint.

Of course, there is this one guy—Zoey's brother, Benjamin.

Yes, he is my sister Claire's boyfriend, but that's a mere technicality. He doesn't really love her. I mean, how could he? We're talking Claire, whose soul is an automatic icemaker. I'm sure that if Benjamin ever thought about it and realized how much I like him, he'd immediately see that we're right for each other.

If he ever even noticed that I'm alive. If he ever bothered for one second to realize that I am not just his buddy, that I am a young woman, and, by the way, not a complete gorgon or

anything. If he ever MANAGED
to pay the SLIGHTEST bit of
attention to the fact that he's
the ONLY guy I've ever been
interested in in my LIFE, the
arrogant, self-centered TOAD . . .

Well, then I think we'd be
just right for each other.

Claire Geiger

I suppose Benjamin is my boy-friend. Either that or he hates me, I'm not sure. And I'm not sure how I feel about him anymore, either. A lot of things are up in the air since I remembered.

See, I honestly didn't remember; that is the truth. You have to under-stand that. For the longest time I tried to remember; at least I believe I tried. I would never have let Lucas go to jail for me. I would never have kept silent for those two years if I'd remembered.

But now I do remember. I was driving the car when Jake's brother, Wade, was killed. Me, not Lucas.

Benjamin suspects the truth. No one knows for sure except me and Lucas and, unfortunately, my father. But Benjamin suspects.

My dad was just trying to protect me. He guessed the truth right from the start, but he made a deal with Lucas and Lucas stuck to it. Why? I don't know. Lucas used to be in love with me, that's one reason. Plus my dad said he'd help Lucas's father out with his business.

And now, if I tell the truth, I don't know what would happen to my father. And if I tell the truth, Jake is sure to turn against me, and I was just starting to realize how much I like him.

But if I don't tell the truth . . . then what kind of a person am I?

Who's my boyfriend? Who's the guy I love? Benjamin? Jake? Is there even some lingering feeling between me and Lucas? Like I said, I don't know anymore.

One

"So, this is your room," Lucas said, letting his dark eyes roam over Zoey's unmade bed, taking in the bookshelves, the journal on her nightstand, the half-open dresser drawer that spilled out white cotton panties and bras.

"This is it." Zoey Passmore waved her arms awkwardly to encompass the room, then let them flop at her sides. Why had she invited him up here? And especially, why had she invited him without bothering to clean up? "Pretty exciting, huh?"

Lucas smiled as Zoey sidled over to close the dresser drawer. "It's been two years since I've been in a girl's room," he said. "It's nice. It smells nice in here."

"It's that subtle interplay between baby powder and dirty laundry," Zoey said.

Lucas leaned into the deep, dormered window. Zoey's father had built a small desk in there where she could do her homework and look down Camden Street, enjoying a view of the slow, gentle life of North Harbor, Chatham

Island's only town. On the right wall of the dormer she tacked notes and lists and reminders about appointments. On the left she put quotations on yellow Post-it notes.

"'Imagination is the eye of the soul,'" Lucas quoted, reading her favorite. "Who is Joseph Joubert?"

Zoey shrugged. "He's the guy who said 'Imagination is the eye of the soul.' That's all I know. I guess maybe someday I should find out."

"I like the quote," Lucas said. He tilted his head sideways. His long, unruly blond hair hung down. "'If there is anything better than to be loved, it is loving,'" he read.

Zoey gulped and felt a blush rising in her cheeks. She ran a hand through her own unruly blond hair. "Yeah, I just, you know . . . kind of liked the way it sounded."

"Anonymous, huh?" He grinned. "Anonymous said a lot of very interesting things."

Zoey laughed. "Yes, he or she has always been one of my favorites."

Lucas stood back, nodding as he looked at her little alcove. "This is how I'll picture you from now on," he said. "Whenever I'm in my room at night, thinking of you, I'll imagine you sitting at this desk, watching the sun setting over the town, the way it is now, and searching for wisdom in quote books." He looked at her with his usual startling, unsettling directness.

"Better than picturing my messy bed, I guess."

Lucas smiled an impish half smile. "Oh, I'll probably think of you there, too," he admitted. "But I'll try to keep those thoughts under control."

"Good," she said.

He reached out for her and she took his hand, just holding the tips of his fingers with hers. For a while that might have been seconds or hours, they just looked at each other. Then Zoey felt his grip tighten on her hand. Lucas drew her to him.

Or perhaps she drew him to her. It was always hard to tell.

His lips met hers, a tender, gentle collision that grew in intensity, escalating so suddenly and explosively that when at last they drew apart, Zoey's lips felt bruised. Her hands shook. Her heart pounded wildly. She could not trust her voice to speak.

The effect Lucas had on her was startling, like nothing she had known before. It was as if she were driving along at ten miles an hour on a quiet street one minute and then, a split second after their lips met, she was doing warp factor nine and blowing past Jupiter. The mental image made her smile.

"It's amazing," Lucas said, grinning a little

foolishly and shaking his head in disbelief.

"You mean—?"

"Kissing you," he said. "It's just . . ." He shook his head again, at a loss for words.

"You too?" Zoey asked shyly. "I thought maybe it was just me."

"Oh, yeah. Like someone shoved a thousand-volt wire up my—" He stopped himself and made a wry face.

"That's a really romantic image," Zoey said, laughing.

"Well, I'm quite a poet," he said self-mockingly.

"Maybe we'd better do it again," she suggested.

"I think we'd better," he agreed.

His lips had just brushed hers when there was a knock at her door.

They flew apart, both looking flustered and guilty.

"Your dad?" Lucas asked in a hoarse whisper.

"He's down at the restaurant," Zoey said. "So's my mom."

The knock came again. "It's just me," a voice said.

Zoey sighed in relief. Benjamin, her older brother. She opened the door. Benjamin slipped inside and closed the door behind him.

"I hope I'm not interrupting anything," he

15

said, turning his dark sunglasses roughly toward the spot where Zoey and Lucas were standing.

"We were . . . uh, going over some homework," Zoey said lamely.

"Of course you were," Benjamin said smoothly. "But in case you weren't just going over your homework, I thought I'd come up and warn you that Jake is downstairs in the family room."

"Jake?" Zoey cried.

"Yeah, you remember," Benjamin said, "your boyfriend? Big guy, muscles, dark hair? He was going to just come on up, but I convinced him you were waxing your legs and you'd be annoyed if he barged in and saw you like that."

"I don't wax my legs," Zoey said.

"It's all I could think of, all right?" Benjamin said. "It was either that or tell him you were up here playing tongue hockey with his worst enemy."

Lucas frowned. "Maybe we should just get this out in the open."

"No!" Zoey said. "I mean, I want to prepare him for it."

"You'll never be able to prepare him for it," Lucas said reasonably.

"He's right," Benjamin said, nodding agreement. "But there might be a gentler way of doing it." Suddenly he froze, cocking his head to listen. "Damn. He's coming."

A second later Zoey heard Jake's quick, heavy tread on the stairs. "Oh, no." She looked pleadingly at Lucas. "Would you mind hiding? Quick?"

Lucas hesitated, as if he might argue, then shook his head in disgust and dropped to the floor, bending over to look under her bed. "What's all this junk under here?"

Jake's tread was closer now, turning the corner at the top of the stairs. "Zo? Are you decent in there?"

"I can't fit under here," Lucas whispered.

"In the closet," Benjamin hissed.

Lucas jumped up, dashed for the closet, slipped inside, and wormed his way back through dresses and jackets and blouses.

Jake knocked on the door. Then, without waiting, he opened it. Zoey's clothes were still rustling and swaying, and far toward the back of the closet, she could still clearly make out a pair of battered leather boots that were definitely not hers.

"Hi, babe," Jake said. He crossed the room to take Zoey in his muscular arms.

"Jake," Zoey said with phony brightness. "Benjamin told me you were here."

"He told me you were waxing your legs," Jake said, giving Benjamin a dubious look.

"I'm all done," Zoey said.

Jake grinned slyly. He hugged her to him and let his hand slip down her side. "Can I feel?" he asked wickedly.

Zoey was sure she saw the boots in her closet begin to move. "No, Jake," she said sharply.

"No, Jake," Benjamin echoed helpfully. "You really shouldn't flirt with my sister while I'm in the room."

And Lucas is in the closet, Zoey added silently.

Jake released her, and Zoey almost sighed in relief. "Are you going to be ready anytime soon?" Jake asked, looking at her skeptically.

"Ready?"

"Yeah, you know. We're all going over to The Tavern for dinner. You, me, my folks."

"That's tonight?" Zoey said, sounding shrill. "But I—I don't have anything to wear to The Tavern." Instantly she saw Benjamin wince and shake his head imperceptibly. Her eyes flew toward the closet.

Jake gave a long-suffering look and marched to the closet.

Oh, no.

"You always say you don't have anything to wear, Zo. How about that blue dress? You know, the one that's got the slit up the side?"

Zoey gulped. She felt frozen in place. Jake was riffling through her clothes now. In a matter of seconds his hand would encounter a warm body amid the silk and cotton.

"Where is that thing?" Jake demanded.

"I . . . I don't think I . . ." Zoey stammered.

"I'm sure it's in here," Jake said. "You know the one I'm talking about." He gathered a bunch of clothes and shifted them to the right.

"Let me!" Zoey yelled, leaping forward.

Jake turned to look over his shoulder.

The dress, the blue dress, suddenly appeared, thrust forward from the back of her closet.

Zoey stretched, shoved past Jake, snatched the dress, and spun to block Jake's view. "Here it is," she said breathlessly.

Jake stared hard.

Zoey felt her smile crumbling.

"Amazing," Jake said. "A girl can just reach right in and find something. I probably could have looked for hours." He clapped Benjamin on the shoulder and laughed. "That's the way it always is. It's the same with a girl's purse."

"Yeah, women," Benjamin said, smiling blandly. "Well, as much fun as it might be to stay, I have to head on over to the Geigers'. Nina's reading for me."

"An evening with *Ninny*," Jake said, making a face. "I thought you could do better than that."

Benjamin shrugged and turned around, walking in his precise way to the head of the stairs. "You shouldn't be jealous just because Nina can read, Jake."

19

Jake laughed good-naturedly and slipped his arm around Zoey's waist. "Hmm. I believe your brother may just have insulted me, Zoey." He drew her close and bent down to kiss her, just as he had so many, many times before.

Zoey reached with her free hand and pushed the closet door.

Her lips opened to Jake.

The door closed on Lucas.

Lucas waited until he heard Jake leave, then stepped out of the closet. Zoey was standing there, holding the blue dress, looking confused and guilty.

Lucas forced a smile. There was no point in making things worse for her.

"I'm so sorry," Zoey whispered.

"You did what you had to," he said flatly.

"I need to tell him," Zoey said, worrying the fabric of the dress in her hands.

Lucas shrugged. "Either that or I'll have to get used to hanging out in closets." He looked at her sideways, told himself not to ask the question that was burning around his brain, then ignored his own good advice. "You kissed him, didn't you?"

Zoey flushed and looked down at the floor.

"Thought so," he said.

"Look, I . . . It was the quickest way to get rid of him," Zoey said.

"And now you're going to spend the night with him and his parents."

"It's something I agreed to a long time ago," Zoey explained. She looked thoroughly miserable, and Lucas told himself to relent. But he couldn't let go of the image of her standing right here, not three feet from him, kissing another guy while Lucas could still taste her lips.

"It's a little hard to take," he said grimly.

"I just need some time, Lucas," Zoey said. She touched his arm. He didn't respond. "You're really mad, aren't you?" she said.

"No," he lied, shaking his head as if it would clear out the disturbing images. Then a more alarming thought occurred to him. "You're not sleeping with him, are you?"

Zoey drew back, arching her eyebrows angrily. "No, Lucas, I'm not. And if I were, which I'm definitely not, do you think I would now? Now that you and I are—"

"Are what?" Lucas said. "That's the question, isn't it? Are we . . . *we*?"

"We're *we*," Zoey said softly.

Lucas tried not to let himself feel too pleased, since he was enjoying feeling resentful, but a wry smile escaped. "You and me?"

"Yes, you and me," Zoey said, smiling shyly.

"No one else?" Lucas demanded.

"I'll tell Jake tonight," Zoey promised. "If, you know, if there's a time when I can do it."

Lucas grimaced at the dress. "That looks kind of low-cut."

Zoey rolled her eyes. "With me, how low-cut could it be? I'm not exactly Claudia Schiffer."

"Too low-cut for Jake," Lucas said grumpily.

"I have to change," Zoey said. "And Jake is still downstairs waiting."

"Sure, go ahead."

"Lucas."

He smiled sheepishly. "I guess you want me to get back in the closet."

"Just turn your head and promise not to peek."

"Okay." He turned away.

"Nice try, Lucas. Turn the other way, *not* toward the mirror."

He laughed. "Mirror? I didn't even notice there was a mirror there." Behind his back he heard the sound of clothing dropping to the floor, of dresser drawers opening and closing, and the sound of silk against skin.

"Ta-daa," Zoey said.

He turned, prepared to make some leering remark, but somehow the sight of her, perfect, so perfect, choked off the words.

"You don't like it?" Zoey asked, looking crestfallen.

"No, it's just . . ." He had to stop and swallow down the lump in his throat. "It's just that you are too beautiful. I can't believe you're real, and that you're mine." As he spoke the words he felt their truth. She *was* too beautiful. Too smart and funny and decent. For him.

Anyone could see that she belonged with Jake, not with him. How could he ever live up to her? What chance was there that this could last? His father was trying to convince his grandfather to take him in, and any day he could be told to go. Was it right to ask Zoey to give up Jake for a guy whose future was an open question?

Zoey laughed self-deprecatingly. She held out her arms and looked down at herself skeptically. "You know, you *have* been living with just guys for the last two years. It obviously doesn't take much to impress you." She gave a twirl, then stopped and looked at him doubtfully. "What's the matter? You look grim."

"Nothing," he said. "I just wanted to say, you know, you can take a while to tell Jake. I'll understand."

"I want to do it as soon as I can," Zoey said. "I want it to be out in the open." She reached for his hand again, and this time he grasped her fingers. "I'll be thinking of you all night."

"Yeah, right," he said, drawing her close.

"Well, just in case, you'd better give me something to remember," she said softly.

He kissed her, feeling waves of desire and pleasure. Waves that almost washed away the lingering realization that these same lips, only moments before, had been on Jake's.

Two

Claire Geiger was walking down Center Street carrying a plastic sack of groceries when she saw Benjamin ahead of her, outlined against a darkening sky as he crossed the street and aimed for her house.

She slowed her pace, hanging back so as not to overtake him. He was using his cane, swinging it from side to side, but only in the most casual manner. North Harbor was such a small town that he had counted out every street and knew exactly how many steps there were from corner to corner.

On this familiar turf Benjamin could move with the easy confidence of a sighted person, lithe and almost graceful. His dark Ray Bans, an integral part of his handsome, serious face, gave him a mysterious, strangely alert look.

Claire held her breath, hoping he didn't know she was here watching him, wondering whether she was ready to talk to him. They hadn't seen each other since he'd told her he knew the truth. That he *thought* he knew the truth.

She made a decision and quickened her pace, breaking into a run to catch him before he reached her gate. "Hey, Benjamin."

Benjamin stopped and turned, his shades aiming just slightly to the left of her. "I was wondering if you were trying to avoid me," he said.

"Avoid you?" She touched his cheek, directing his mouth, and kissed him lightly on the lips.

"Yes. You know, when you stopped by the kite shop." He smiled his knowing half smile. "You have a distinctive walk, Claire. And you're wearing thongs. You can't sneak around when you're wearing thongs."

Claire laughed as nonchalantly as she could. "You know, most girls would think the cool thing about having a boyfriend who's blind would be that he couldn't keep track of them. But, of course, they'd be wrong about that."

"Actually, I think what most girls would like about a blind boyfriend is that he would never know if they were beautiful or not." He reached toward her, letting his hand drift slowly at the right height, till his fingers touched her face. "Although I hear that's not something you'd ever have to worry about, Claire." He looked at her wistfully. "Eyes as dark as your hair, Zoey tells me. But then, I still remember that from when we were little."

"Were you heading over to my house to see me?" Claire asked, sidestepping his compliment. People had told her all her life she was beautiful. Her relationship with Benjamin had been one of the few she'd had where her looks played no great role.

"Yes."

"Just dropping by?" she asked, trying to make the question sound innocent.

"Nina's going to read to me," he said. "And I wanted to talk to you."

An island car went by, rattling along the cobblestones, its punctured muffler roaring.

"Let's go down to the rocks for a minute," Claire suggested. "Nina will wait."

"All right," Benjamin said.

They walked the few yards to the end of the street and crossed Lighthouse Road. Claire kicked off her thongs and climbed out onto one of the many tumbled boulders that lined the shore at the northern tip of the island. Benjamin could only follow slowly. He used his cane to outline the nearest boulder, carefully defining the angle of its surfaces. Then he stuck out his left foot, felt the hard surface with the toe of his sneaker, and hopped onto it.

He stayed on a flat rock while Claire set down her bag of groceries and climbed a little farther out. The sea was calm, just a low swell running past the point, crashing and receding

26

in quick, hushed strokes. The tidal pools formed by the crevices of the rocks rose and fell, but only gently.

Definitely a front coming in, Claire noticed, with her usual keen attention to the sky. A line of red and gold-trimmed clouds off to the south-west was advancing, as if fleeing the dying sun. There might be rain, she realized, possibly even a small storm. A storm would be nice.

"I haven't seen you all weekend," Benjamin said. Claire was startled to hear his voice so close by. He had managed to work his way out to her and now stood confidently on a slanted slab of granite. One pants leg was wet from a misstep along the way.

"I didn't realize I was obligated to see you every day," Claire said.

"You're not. It's just that the last time I saw you . . . well, you were reeling around the room and acting like the world was coming to an end."

"Oh, that," Claire said dismissively. "I was just woozy. I had a lousy night's sleep the night before, and I'd swiped a beer from the refrigerator before coming over."

"So that's all it was," Benjamin said, sounding neither skeptical nor convinced. "I thought maybe your reaction had something to do with my little theory."

"Theory?" Claire said, trying to keep from

sounding brittle. Benjamin had a deadly accurate ability to read tone of voice.

"Yeah. My theory that you were the one driving the car when Wade McRoyan was killed. That theory. Slipped your mind, huh?"

"No, it didn't slip my mind. And really, the truth is, Benjamin, it shook me up for a while. As you know, I've never remembered what happened that night, so I began to wonder if maybe you were right. I had to ask myself if it was possible." She watched his reaction closely. The subtle superior smile faded. His jaw tightened. Claire grinned triumphantly. *Yes, I thought that might be the way to handle you, Benjamin.*

"You're saying you still don't remember?"

"No, I don't," Claire said. "Which doesn't necessarily mean you're wrong, Benjamin. You may even be right. Maybe it *was* me driving drunk that night. For that matter, maybe it was Wade himself." *There, let it go,* Claire told herself sternly. *Don't try to push it. Don't overdo it.*

It was always a chess match with Benjamin. She had to be on guard all the time, particularly when she wanted to deceive him. He was not a guy who could be misled by an innocent look or a pretty smile.

She had turned him aside for now, but she could tell Benjamin was far from convinced. In the end, if she was going to keep her secret, she would have to get him out of her life.

Benjamin started to say something, then stopped. His brow furrowed in concentration. Claire could see herself reflected in his black sunglasses. At last his brow cleared. "Claire, if you did remember . . ."

"Yes?"

"If you did remember, and what you remembered was that it was you, and not Lucas, who was driving the car, would you tell?"

Claire stared straight into the distorted reflection of her own face. "Yes, Benjamin. Of course I would. What kind of person do you think I am?"

A ghost of a smile formed on his lips. "I don't know, Claire. Do you?"

Nina looked from her window and saw Benjamin and her sister, side by side, coming across the road from the water. They were holding hands. Claire was carrying a bag of groceries. Benjamin was carrying her thongs.

Nina glanced at the clock beside her bed. He was fifteen minutes late.

Fifteen minutes. Well, fine, if he wanted to run around with Claire and waste fifteen minutes. She still got paid by the hour to read homework to him, and she was going to charge the Passmores for the fifteen minutes. After all, she could have used the time doing something else. She was a busy girl. It wasn't like she was just waiting around for Benjamin to show up so she could read to him.

Wasn't like that at all. She had a life.

And if he spent the next ten minutes downstairs making out with Claire, fine, she'd charge his parents for that time, too. Five dollars an hour. Ten minutes of making out, that would cost them . . . ten minutes was one sixth of an hour, into five . . . it would cost him about eighty-three cents. Maybe she would just point that out to him.

She grabbed the bottle of *Escape* she'd bought at Porteous and sprayed a little on her wrists. She smelled it, shrugged, and checked herself in the mirror. She looked okay, in a great shirt she'd picked up at the Goodwill thrift shop in Weymouth, under a loose-fitting army shirt and shorts. She shoved her dark hair into approximately the right location. Pointless, really, since for all Benjamin knew she could be wearing a clown suit and a Bozo wig. But maybe the perfume would get his attention. After all, he could still smell.

He knocked at her door.

"Come in," she said loudly.

He opened the door and stood there. "Is it safe for me to come in? I mean, have you strewn your floor with clothes like last time?"

"No, the floor is clear," she said sharply, bending down quickly to snatch a single boot and a bag of Doritos out of his path. "You're late, you know."

"Sorry."

"I do have a life, you realize."

Benjamin tilted his head at her quizzically. "Are you in a bad mood? We could make this another time."

"No," Nina said quickly. "No. Let's do it now. Sorry I snapped."

Benjamin made his way to her bed and sat down on the edge, then pushed off his sneakers and lifted his feet, making himself comfortable. He handed her a book. "It's poetry. Sorry about that."

Nina rolled her eyes to the ceiling and shook her fist at an invisible fate. She hated reading poetry. She could never get the rhythm right. And Benjamin would correct her. *No, it's supposed to be accented on the third syllable.* It was so much harder than just regular reading. She hated it. "No problem," she said.

"Thanks," Benjamin said. "We're supposed to read Shelley."

Nina made a face and silently mimicked, *We're supposed to read Shelley.* We were supposed to read Shelley fifteen minutes ago, but you were too busy playing slippery lippery with the ice princess.

"Percy Bysshe Shelley."

Percy Bysshe Shelley, Nina mimicked. *Why*

31

don't you get Claire to read Percy Bysshe Shelley to you? She turned to the table of contents, found the right section, and dragged her chair over by the bed.

Benjamin frowned. "Is that . . . is that perfume?"

Finally. He noticed. "Um, I guess so. I mean, someone gave me some, and, you know, I may have spilled it or something."

"Hmm," he said.

Hmm? Hmm? That was it? Forty-two dollars on her dad's charge account for *Hmm*?

"Does it bother you?" she asked.

"Naw. It smells a little like melons, doesn't it? I think the poem is called Indian something."

Nina gritted her teeth and considered giving Benjamin the finger, but that seemed mean. It wasn't nice to take advantage of the fact that he couldn't see. Then she did it anyway, because it made her feel good. Then she did it with both hands because that made her feel even better.

She began to read.

> *I arise from dreams of thee*
> *In the first sleep of night—*
> *The winds are breathing low*
> *And the stars are burning bright.*

It was a love poem, Nina realized. She

looked sharply at Benjamin. A love poem? Was this really on the senior curriculum, or could it be possible that he was trying to tell her something?

> *I arise from dreams of thee—*
> *And a spirit in my feet*
> *Has borne me—Who knows how?*
> *To thy chamber window, sweet!—*

Wait a minute. Here he was, *in* her chamber. Okay, probably just a coincidence, but still, the *first* thing he'd asked her to read was a love poem.

> *The wandering airs they faint*
> *On the dark silent stream—*
> *The champak odours fail . . .*

"Champak?" Benjamin asked.

"That's what it says," Nina said. "Champak."

"Would you mind looking it up?"

Nina got up and rummaged on her bookshelf for the dictionary. "Champak. It's some kind of tree that has fragrant flowers."

"Oh," Benjamin said. "Maybe that's where your perfume came from."

Nina smiled. That was better than *Hmm*. He was relating the poem to her. She hurried through the rest of the second verse, which had somehow dragged a dead nightingale into the story. But the third verse was better.

> *O lift me from the grass!*
> *I die, I faint, I fail!*
> *Let thy love in kisses rain*
> *On my lips and eyelids pale.*

Okay, this was definitely a love poem. And was it just her imagination, or was Benjamin listening to her more attentively than usual? Especially around the *kisses raining on my lips* part.

> *My cheek is cold and white, alas!*
> *My heart beats loud and fast.*

Nina gulped. Actually, her heart *was* beating fast. She shifted in her seat. It had to be deliberate. Benjamin was amazingly subtle, for a guy. He had to have known that having her read a poem like this, full of kisses and champak odors, while he lay back on her very bed . . .

> *O press it close to thine own again*
> *Where it will break at last.*

Benjamin nodded thoughtfully. "You're getting better at reading poetry. You got some real feeling into that."

Nina swallowed hard. "Well, it was more about something I . . . you know, I mean, it was more about . . ." She was sinking into her seat, her voice growing lower as she sank.

You're mumbling, Nina! she chided herself. *Why are you mumbling? You never mumble with anyone else. Stop mumbling and spit it out.*

"You mean it's something you identify with more," Benjamin said helpfully.

"I guess so," Nina mumbled.

"It's a love poem," Benjamin said.

"Yeah, I kind of thought so, too," Nina managed to say.

Benjamin smiled. "I never thought of you as a romantic type, Nina. Is it anyone in particular, or is that none of my business?"

Anyone in particular? Had he already guessed? Was he just waiting, hoping that she would tell him how she truly felt about him?

It was the perfect opening, the perfect opportunity. He'd asked her to read a love poem, then he'd asked her if it meant anything special to her. Plus, he loved her perfume. Or at least he had noticed it.

All she had to do now was open her mouth and say, Benjamin, I am totally in love with you. All she had to do was open her mouth and say—

"Benjamin?"

"Yes?"

35

"I . . . I . . . was just wondering what you'd like me to read next."

Claire paused at the door to Nina's room. She could hear her sister's voice droning on and Benjamin's occasional interruptions. Good. They would be busy for the next hour at least, then probably Benjamin would stay for dinner.

She mounted the stairs to the next level, her room, perched alone atop the house. There was a small metal box on her desk, a miniature weather station that gave temperature and wind and barometer readings. She noted the information with satisfaction.

Then she climbed the ladder that ran up one wall, pushed open the trapdoor, and climbed out onto the widow's walk. It was her favorite place in the world, quiet, inviolate, with a view of the town, the island, the water, and the overarching sky. It was the reason she loved this house. The reason she would have a hard time leaving it to go away to college.

The sun was dying over Weymouth, turning the tall buildings there into black rectangles of shadow, turning the water red.

She walked to the west end of the widow's walk to the tall brick chimney that rose beside it and quickly found the right brick. It came out easily. Claire reached inside the hole and pulled out a small leather book.

Claire glanced down at the yard, though she knew it was empty and that no one could have seen her behind the chimney anyway. She sat down on the roof, leaned back against the railing, pulled a pen from the pocket of her jeans, and opened the book to the next empty page.

She put the date and the time at the top of the page. Then the temperature and the wind's speed and direction.

Diary:

There appears to be a front moving in from the west-southwest. But the barometer is only dropping slowly, so we're probably not in for a storm.

On the personal front

She sighed and looked down at the challenging blank page. This was a momentous entry, probably an ending to a long chapter in her life.

I had a talk with Benjamin just a few minutes ago. I think I've thrown him off for now. I told him I still didn't remember anything. I don't know if he believed me or not. He is pretty good at hiding his true feelings. I've never even really known how he feels about me.

Something we have in common, maybe, an ability to keep our private lives private.

Maybe that's why I've been thinking more about Jake lately. Maybe because he wouldn't be constantly trying to dig below the surface like Benjamin. My relationship with Benjamin can be exhausting at times.

38

"But that's not the real problem," Claire said aloud. "It's not just about whether I end it with Benjamin or not." As sad as that thought made her, it was only part of the problem.

But that's not the real problem. The real problem is, What do I do now that I remember what happened that night? Do I tell the truth, or do I keep up the lie?

If I keep lying, it hurts Lucas. And I guess it hurts Zoey, too, because I'm pretty sure she's falling for Lucas. She thinks she's keeping it secret, and I guess she is from Jake, but Jake's just a guy and not the most perceptive guy on earth, either.

If I tell the truth, I hurt myself.

People would be convinced I'd been lying all along. They'd be sure I deliberately let Lucas go to jail to protect me.

And there's Dad. He says what he did, offering Lucas's father help with his business, would look like a bribe, or perjury or whatever.

So I can either hurt Lucas and Zoey, or I can hurt my dad and me.

I want to do what's right.

She closed the book. "What's right," she sneered. She knew perfectly well what was right. The right thing was to tell the truth. But was it the smart thing to do? After all, Lucas had already suffered, and there wasn't anything she could do about that. How would it help for her to suffer as well, and maybe drag her father into too? In his business, reputation was important.

She opened the book.

But what is right? Is Zoey's little flirtation with Lucas really more important than my own father? Besides, Lucas came out of it okay. Maybe he's got some problems with his family—who doesn't? And it's not like Lucas was ever a plaster saint.

If I keep quiet, everyone survives okay. The only real trouble comes if I open my big mouth.

She closed the book and stood up. It wasn't a pleasant decision, but it was the smart decision, she told herself. She hid the diary again, replacing the brick.

Which left only the question of Benjamin.

Benjamin would have to go. He was too hard to deceive, too dangerous to have around. The realization gave her a sharp stab of pain. Benjamin had been part of her life for a long time. He was so much like her in many ways: private, aloof, independent, difficult, challenging.

Relentless when he wanted something. And he wanted the truth.

When she thought of Jake, the whole picture changed. Being with him would be so easy. And she had always been attracted to him. It wasn't like this was a sudden decision, not really. She'd thought of him often. Sooner or later Zoey would drop Jake. And then Claire could pick him up.

Her lies would go on unchallenged and everyone would be happy. Except, of course, for Benjamin.

Nina

Okay, picture me in fifth grade. Braces, hair from hell, clothes from the Miss Young Dork collection, zero buffers, permanent nose zit. Such a dweeb even I didn't want to hang out with me.

Still, there was this guy named Sketch. Really, I wouldn't make that up; his mom was an artist. He had a brother named Canvas. Anyway, I was in major love with Sketch, who was in sixth grade but was held back in my math class. I drew little hearts on my notebook with "Sketch and Nina" inside. I held imaginary conversations wherein I would try out lines like, "Meet my boyfriend, Sketch," or "Allow me to introduce my husband, Sketch."

Often I would become distracted and start coming up with sentences like, "This is Sketch, he's a bit of a lech, but he's fetched a job as a sketch artist in Saskatchewan."

But to get back to the point, which is my pathetic love life. Sketch seemed somewhat unaware of my love for him. In fact, he seemed somewhat unaware that I was alive. So I

decided to come up with a fool-
proof plan to make him love me.
It had five steps:

1. Try to sit next to him at lunch.
2. Let him copy off my math tests.
3. Always smile at him but don't
   show braces.
4. Try to run into him at the mall.
5. Get Claire to find out if he
   likes me.

I didn't have much success
with steps one through four.
But five worked beautifully.
Claire agreed to find out if he
liked me.

He didn't.

He did, however, like Claire,

who was his same age and had no braces, no zits, perfect hair, and the Grand Tetons.

All of which taught me one very important thing. I should have come straight out with it and told Sketch how I felt.

It probably wouldn't have worked any better, but at least he wouldn't have ended up going out with my sister.

Three

"Wait a minute," Aisha Gray said. "You had Lucas in the closet."

"Yes."

"And Jake in your room," Nina said, giving Aisha a sly look. She shook her head and took a drag on the never-lit cigarette stuck in the corner of her mouth. "And here Aisha and I don't have even *one* boyfriend between us."

"It wasn't a moment to be proud of," Zoey said darkly.

They were standing together at the stern railing of the *Minnow*, the ferry that ran from the islands, Chatham, Allworthy, and Penobscot, to the mainland city of Weymouth, where all the island kids of high school age attended school. It was a gray, overcast, chilly morning, too chilly for the second week of September, but then, Maine could grow cold without warning.

Zoey looked over her shoulder at the rest of their friends. Claire sat reading her history book, her long, glossy black hair lifting in the

47

breeze. Benjamin sat beside her, tilting his head to better hear the cries of the gulls floating along in the air beside the ferry. He smiled as a wisp of Claire's hair floated across his face.

To their right, up in the front corner of the open deck, sat Jake, staring stonily ahead, arms spread across the bench back, feet propped on the railing.

Lucas was in the far-left corner reading a book, occasionally combing his hair back with his fingers.

Zoey shook her head and sighed.

"Yeah, things have changed," Nina said, as though Zoey had spoken aloud. "Used to be we all sat together, more or less."

"The good old days of last week," Aisha said.

Zoey bit her lip. Aisha did not approve of her decision to be with Lucas. She thought Zoey should be able to control her romantic impulses. Aisha was taller and thinner than either Zoey or Nina, with an explosion of long, springy hair pulled back from her skeptical, high-cheekboned face. She used her extra inch of height to look down, arms crossed over her chest, shaking her head at Zoey's folly.

"And you haven't even told Jake yet," Aisha added in a low whisper. "You need to tell him, Zoey. It's only fair. You should have told him already."

"I'm going to go sit down," Nina said.

"No," Zoey said, grabbing her friend's arm. "You guys have to stay here with me. If we sit down, I'll have to either sit with Jake, which will hurt Lucas's feelings, or else sit with Lucas."

"Which will start World War III," Nina said.

"If we just stand here and look like we're talking about girl stuff, neither of them will care."

"Girl stuff?" Nina turned the phrase over. "Girl stuff? You mean like we should be discussing our favorite brand of tampon or something?"

"Or we could all just huddle together and giggle," Aisha suggested acerbically.

Zoey rolled her eyes. "Look, we can talk about peace in the Middle East if you want, just so long as neither guy thinks I'm avoiding him."

"See, this is what I said would happen when you started fooling around, Zoey," Aisha said. "Now Nina and I are dragged into it and everyone is lying to everyone else."

"You don't have to lie," Zoey said, stung by Aisha's words.

"You're lying to Jake, Nina and I are lying to Jake and Claire, Benjamin knows, so he's obviously lying to Claire, too. Lucas is lying by pretending he doesn't care about you. I mean, jeez, Zoey. A week ago we were all close friends who more or less told each other the truth."

"More or less," Nina added.

"Look, I'll tell Jake soon," Zoey said. "I promise."

"Like that will fix everything right up," Aisha muttered. "You're going to dump a guy you've been going with forever so you can be with a guy who, according to you, is about to get shipped out of town by his own father. People get led around by their hormones, and this is what happens."

"So," Nina said brightly, "let's talk about tampons."

"Aisha, just because you have no romance in your soul doesn't mean that those of us who do are idiots," Zoey said defensively. Too much of what Aisha was saying was hitting home.

"But you have *two* romances in your soul at the same time," Nina pointed out.

Zoey hung her head. They were right. She was putting her friends in an awkward position. She was forcing them to choose between her, on the one hand, and Jake and Claire on the other. And worse than that, she was basically making a fool out of Jake behind his back. Plus forcing Lucas to deny his own feelings.

She raised her head. "Please, you guys, I know this is bogus, but I need your help. Just until I tell Jake, which I promise will be soon."

"Look," Nina said, nudging Aisha. "She's got a tear in her eye. Right there in the corner."

"That is so manipulative," Aisha said, shaking her head. "I'll bet she can't squeeze it out."

"I wish I could do that," Nina said. "The ability to generate tears is very useful."

"Yeah, it works even on me," Aisha admitted. "All right, Zoey, cut it out. I'm not mad at you, I'm just saying you should focus more on controlling your emotions."

Zoey smiled and wiped away the tear. "You know something, Eesh? You talk tough, but someday you're going to fall so hard over some guy it's going to be pathetic to watch."

"Not me," Aisha said confidently.

"It's Jake," Nina hissed. "He's coming over, and Lucas is watching him."

Zoey kept her gaze focused away. She made quick eye contact with Nina and Aisha. Aisha nodded imperceptibly.

"No, no, I really prefer the plastic applicator," Aisha said.

"But they're not biodegradable," Zoey argued loudly.

"Hey," Nina nearly shouted. "What's the matter with good, old-fashioned Kotex? I'm talking maxipads, big, thick, like walking around with a mattress down your panties."

From the corner of her eye Zoey saw Jake freeze. His lip curled; he made a disgusted face and veered away.

"Gets 'em every time," Zoey said. "Now, getting back to peace in the Middle East . . ."

Jake stopped at midcourt, dribbling the basketball and looking over the defenders. Well, well, he was in luck. Lucas was right between him and the basket.

"Move the ball, McRoyan!" Coach Zane yelled from the sidelines. This was just regular gym class, but Coach Zane also coached the varsity basketball team, and he had been trying for some time to get Jake to abandon football in favor of basketball.

Jake saw one of his teammates running a pattern that would set him up perfectly for a pass, but Jake didn't want to pass. He wanted to take the ball to the net himself. And he wanted to take it right through Lucas Cabral.

He made his move, plowing forward, big, unstoppable, aiming straight for Lucas. Jake dropped his shoulder, football style, and hit Lucas squarely in the chest. Lucas was knocked back, falling spread-eagle toward the hardwood floor.

But as Lucas fell, his foot lashed out. Probably just an accident, Jake realized; still, it landed with deadly accuracy. Jake took two more steps before the pain hit him. He let the ball roll free and doubled over, clutching at himself.

"Foul!" Coach Zane yelled. "Come on,

McRoyan, this ain't football. You can't just hit a man." He came running over and looked down at Jake, now on his knees. "You all right? Serves you right, taking a cheap shot. Okay, that's the period, hit the showers," he said as Jake got to his feet.

The thirty guys in the class all ran for the showers, stripping off sweaty shirts and shorts the minute they were inside.

"You gonna live, Jake?" Lars Ehrlich asked, grinning as he twirled the combination to his gym locker.

Jake gave him a sour look. "I wish I knew whether that was deliberate," Jake said, glaring across the room at Lucas, who had slipped under the shower head and was lathering a bar of soap.

Jake removed the rest of his gym clothes, stuffed them loosely in the bottom of his locker, and headed for the shower himself. Lucas moved away as he approached.

Jake snorted. Probably afraid Jake was going to start something. But no, he'd promised Zoey he wouldn't go after Lucas, no matter how sick it made him to have to be in the same room with the guy.

"Don't worry, killer," Jake said. "I'm not going to hurt you."

Everyone in the shower room instantly shut up and all eyes turned toward Lucas. Lucas stuck his head under the spray and said nothing.

"Looks to me like he's ignoring you," Lars said.

Jake watched Lucas closely. It was possible that kick had been deliberate, which meant Lucas could be fast and accurate, even while falling. Still, Jake had thirty or forty pounds on him.

"He's afraid if he tries to say anything, he'll burst out crying," Jake said dismissively.

Lucas squeezed the water out of his hair and met Jake's eye. He seemed to be debating with himself, then shrugged and shook his head. He walked out of the shower, picked up his towel, and slung it over his shoulder.

After he'd dressed he came back toward Jake and planted himself squarely, feet wide apart, in front of Jake's locker.

Jake finished buttoning his shirt and faced him, hands loose at his sides.

"I've really been hoping we wouldn't have to go through this, Jake," Lucas said in a low voice. "But you're the kind of guy who just won't let things go."

"Things? You mean like I should just get over the fact that you killed my brother?"

"I'll say this once. There were three of us in that car, and all three of us were drunk. I pleaded guilty and I've done my time, and it's over."

Jake felt anger boiling up inside him. "I promised someone I wouldn't beat the crap out of you," he said through gritted teeth.

"Don't let that stop you," Lucas said.

Jake clenched his fist, but then, with an effort, he relaxed. He smiled coldly. "You're not worth it. You're gone, anyway. Your own father is kicking you out."

"Zoey told you that?" Lucas demanded sharply.

It took several seconds for the implication of Lucas's question to sink in. *Zoey told you that? Zoey?*

"Your father let my dad know he was shipping you off," Jake explained in a halting, disconnected voice. His brow was deeply furrowed, but his eyes unfocused. "What was that about Zoey?"

"Nothing," Lucas said, but his eyes betrayed the truth.

"You've been talking to Zoey?"

"Who I talk to is none of your business."

"You son of a bitch."

"She's not your property, Jake."

Jake swung fast, but wild. Lucas caught his fist against his right arm, then drove his own fist into Jake's neck. Jake gasped for air, choking, and a second blow caught him in the stomach, doubling him over. He sank to his knees on the tile. Lucas stood over him, a cold look in his eyes. Jake reached to grab him, but Lucas backed away, out of range.

"I gave you one free shot last week on the

ferry," Lucas said. "Don't try me again, Jake. I've spent the last two years with a very unfriendly crowd, learning how to take care of myself. Don't push me too far." He turned and walked out the door.

Jake got up, feeling humiliated and furious.

"He sucker-punched you," Brian McNeil said.

"You'll get him next time," Lars said sympathetically.

Jake nodded and leaned his head against his locker. His stomach hurt, but he would survive that. Worse by far was the growing realization of what was happening. Zoey wasn't just *talking* to Lucas.

She's not your property, Jake, Lucas had said.

Impossible. Could Zoey actually be interested in Lucas? Was she actually seeing Lucas behind his back? His worst enemy? No, that was impossible. Not Zoey. She wouldn't do that to him. He was imagining things.

With numb, unfeeling hands he closed his locker. The room was emptying as guys went off to their next classes.

Zoey and Lucas? He had to know. Even the faint suspicion was too much to bear. He had to know.

Four

"Oh, brown goo on white bread, my favorite," Nina said, looking down at her lunch tray.

"I think it's turkey," Zoey said doubtfully. "You can tell by the peas. Turkey always comes with peas. If it was Salisbury steak, there would be gray beans."

"Where is Salisbury, anyway, and why do they force their steaks on the rest of the world?" Aisha demanded.

"Salisbury's not far from Turkey," Nina said. "And you two are supposed to be seniors. Pay attention during geography, and you'd know that Turkey is separated from Salisbury by Greece."

"Greece," Zoey groaned. "That's bad."

"Yes, and Frankfurt and Hamburg aren't in Germany, either," Nina said, grinning mischievously. "Nope. They're in Ireland."

"Ireland? I don't get it," Zoey said.

"Actually, in County *Mayo*, Ireland. Mayo. Get it?"

"Now I get it," Zoey said darkly. "I wish I hadn't."

"She gets it, she just doesn't relish it," Aisha added.

"Please stop," Zoey said politely. "I'm armed with red Jell-O. Don't make me use it."

They paid for their lunches and headed toward a vacant table. Zoey noticed Claire coming out of the other lunch line. "Hey, Claire," Zoey said quickly before Nina could poke her in the ribs, "would you like to join us in our sumptuous feast?"

"Sure," Claire said unenthusiastically. It was an unwritten rule between Nina and Claire that they spent as little time near each other as possible while they were at school. But Zoey had felt there was some undefined tension between herself and Claire. It had been evident on the ferry ride that morning. And Aisha's warning about the group becoming divided had hit home with Zoey. The island kids had always hung together.

She caught sight of Lucas, sitting several tables away at a discreet distance. He looked even more solemn and withdrawn than usual.

"Are you going to eat that?" Claire asked Nina as they sat down. "I thought you weren't eating anything that involved animal flesh."

Nina shrugged. "I'm starting with cows and pigs. I'll work my way down to chickens and turkeys."

"How about fish?" Aisha asked.

"That's stage three," Nina said.

"Stage four is you starve to death," Claire said. "You know, this vegetarian thing is—"

"Uh-oh," Aisha murmured.

Zoey felt a hard tap on her shoulder and turned around in annoyance. Jake stood over her, looking huge, his face distorted by cold anger.

"Hi, Jake," Zoey said.

"I need to talk to you," Jake said in a low, dangerous voice.

"Um, okay, pull up a chair," Zoey said.

"Alone. Now."

"Jake, I'm eating—" She gestured vaguely toward her tray.

"I don't give a damn about your food," Jake snapped. "I want to know what's going on, Zoey."

Zoey felt the hush that was falling over the lunchroom, a ripple of whispers and strained attention. Nina and Aisha's eyes were aimed down at the table. Claire watched with calm detachment, her dark-in-dark eyes curious and alert.

"What are you talking about?" Zoey asked, buying precious time.

"You and Lucas," Jake said. "I'm talking about you and Lucas. You and that dirtbag."

Zoey felt her throat clenching up. Everyone was staring at her. She glanced toward Lucas and met his eye. He was grim, waiting for her to answer.

She hung her head and answered in a whisper. "Jake, I was going to tell you—"

Jake interrupted with a string of expletives, slamming his fist onto the table. He started to walk away but instantly turned back. Zoey flinched. Lucas started to rise from his seat.

"Why?" Jake demanded. His eyes were wide, but no longer with rage. Now they pleaded, and Zoey felt like she'd been stabbed in the heart. "Why would you do this to me?"

"Jake—" she began desperately.

"I love you, Zo. We've been together since . . . forever, it seems like. I thought you loved me, too."

"I . . . I do. I mean, I did." The final word came out in a barely audible whisper. "I didn't mean to hurt you."

"Didn't mean—" He smiled a desolate, desperate smile, and to Zoey's horror she saw that there were tears in his eyes. He tried to speak, but the words wouldn't come out. He stood there, his big body seeming strangely shrunken and sagging.

"Jake," Zoey said. But there was nothing else for her to say.

He looked at her hopefully, as if she might still change her mind and tell him it was all just a terrible joke. At last he turned away.

A thundering silence followed him as he strode from the room. Then a nervous laugh from somewhere in the crowd. And whispers that rapidly grew in volume.

Lucas sat with his head in his hands, looking nearly as unhappy as Jake. Even Nina looked at Zoey with accusing eyes.

"I didn't think . . ." Zoey began helplessly. "I never wanted to hurt him. I loved him. I still do, it's just . . ." Zoey bit her knuckles. Nothing like this had ever happened to her. People were staring at her, no doubt thinking she was the bitch of all time. Then another thought occurred to her. "How did he find out? Did one of you tell him?"

Aisha gave her a dirty look. "Don't take it out on us, Zoey. As of right now, the three of us are the only friends you've got."

Claire stood up slowly, lifting her tray. "Make that two."

Dear Jake:
I'm writing you this letter because the truth is, I'm afraid to try to talk to you. Not that I'm saying I'm afraid of you, because of course I'm not.

61

Dear Jake:

I know this probably seems strange, me writing you this letter. I'm going to ask Nina or Aisha to bring it to you because I want you to get it right away. I just want to try to explain, and I know that if I went over and saw you right now that we'd end up arguing. I don't blame you for hating me.

Dear Jake:

Look, I'm sorry about the way things worked out, but I can't help how I feel, any more than you can help how you feel. Which I guess is pretty mad right now. I didn't deliberately try to humiliate

62

Dear Jake:
First of all, I am so
sorry. So very sorry. Lucas
explained to me what hap-
pened

Dear Jake:
First of all, I'm sorry
about how things turned
out. I was a thoughtless
jerk not to let you know
in some kinder way. I am
ashamed of myself and I
probably feel as bad
about this as you do.
Honestly, I don't think
I've even felt so down and
depressed.
You and I were together
a long, long time, Jake, and
I hope you know I'll
always love you

Dear Jake:

First of all, I'm sorry about how things turned out. I was a thoughtless jerk not to let you know in some kinder way. I am ashamed of myself and I probably feel as bad about this as you do. Honestly, I don't think I've ever felt so down and depressed.

You and I were together a long, long time, Jake, and I hope you know I'll always care for you as a close friend. You and I have done so much together and been so much to each other. I also hope that someday you will forgive me for hurting you.

If I could have somehow

stopped feeling for Lucas
the way I

Dear Jake:
I've tried to write this
letter about ten times and
it keeps coming out wrong.
I keep trying to find some
way to ask you to forgive me.
But I guess that's really
just selfish of me. You're
mad at me and I deserve
it. I should have been more
up-front. I know it still
would have hurt you, but
the way I handled it makes
me feel like scum. Sorry.
You know me well enough
after all the time we've
spent together that you
can probably guess I'm
crying as I write this. I
hate hurting people, espe-

cially a person I will always, always care about.

Maybe I'm just losing my mind. I know I didn't plan for any of this to happen. Now that it has happened, I can't stand thinking of the pain I've caused you. It's tearing me up inside.

I don't want you to hate me, and I also don't want you to hate Lucas. I want somehow for every-thing to be all right and back to normal, with all of us being friends, friends like we were a long, long time ago, before everything happened.

I'm writing this because I know if I call you on the phone, I'll just end up blubbering. And I'm asking Nina or Aisha to take it over to you right away so that at least you'll know I'm thinking about you, and caring about you and wishing there were some way for me to make the pain go away.

I guess that's all I have to say, Jake. Except that I really did love you all those times I said I did. And I really am sorry that I changed.

Your friend,
Zoey

Zoey grabbed a tissue from the box of Puffs on her desk and pressed it against her streaming eyes. Nina leaned over her shoulder and read the letter silently.

"I feel like crap," Zoey said through the tissue.

"It's a good letter," Nina said thoughtfully. Zoey felt the pressure of Nina's hand on her shoulder. Then Nina picked up the letter and handed it to Aisha, who was sitting on Zoey's bed.

Aisha read it over and handed it back to Nina. "It's nice, Zoey. It's about all you can do, except for dumping Lucas real fast and going back to Jake."

"I can't do that," Zoey said, wiping her eyes dry with a second tissue. "I think I'm really in love with Lucas."

Aisha seemed to be biting her tongue.

"I know what you're going to say, Eesh," Zoey said, breathing deep to clear away the sobs. "I thought I was in love with Jake, too."

"Well, you have to admit, you are a little unreliable on this," Aisha said. "What is different about the way you feel with Lucas? I mean, is it just exactly like Jake, only ten percent more or something?"

Zoey shrugged. "I don't know. I always really liked Jake. I always thought he was really good-looking and sexy."

Nina shivered and made a face. "Don't mention the words sexy and Jake in the same sentence."

"I think he's sexy," Aisha said. "I'd go along with that. Maybe a good solid eight on a scale of ten."

"It's not that I suddenly didn't like Jake anymore," Zoey said. "It's just that all of a sudden there was Lucas. And it was like . . ." She searched her mind for a comparison. "It was like, you know, how at night the moon can seem amazingly bright, but then you get days when the moon is still up in the sky, but the sun is up, too? And then the moon looks pale and the sun looks so incredibly bright?"

"So Jake is the moon and Lucas is the sun," Nina said dryly. "Zoey, have you been working on your romance novel again?"

"Which one of us is supposed to deliver this letter to Jake?" Aisha asked unenthusiastically.

"I don't want to do it," Nina said.

"You think *I* do?" Aisha asked.

"I'll flip you for it," Nina said, pulling a quarter from her pocket.

"I hope you know what you're doing, Zoey," Aisha said.

"I do," Zoey said, trying to sound confident. "I've learned my lesson. I want to get it all out in the open. That's the only way things will ever get better."

"I meant that I hope you know what you're doing, choosing Lucas over Jake," Aisha said.

"I know what I feel in my heart," Zoey said softly, but with conviction.

"Call it," Nina said, tossing the coin in the air.

Claire

Here's something that Zoey never found out: I had already kissed Jake, long before the two of them broke up.

It was just last year, Christmas vacation. Zoey and Benjamin had gone off with their parents to stay with their grandparents for a week. While they were gone, we got about a foot of new snow. I happened to run into Jake, who was roaring around the beach on a snowmobile his dad had just bought. Being Jake, he didn't offer me a ride because, after all, what would Zoey think if she found out?

So I asked him, and he couldn't
really refuse. We paced on down
along the beach, half a mile or more,
kicking up a big plume of snow
while the surf crashed just beside us,
me holding on to him from behind.

He stopped after a while and said
something about how cold it was. He
said his lips were frozen stiff. So I
said I'd have to do something about
that.

The kiss lasted maybe one second.
No big deal to me, just a whim, but
you would have thought Jake had
been caught selling crack to five-
year-olds inside a church. He made
me swear ten times I wouldn't ever

tell Zoey. It could never happen again, he was faithful, he was in love with Zoey, blah, blah, blah.

I was a little insulted, to be honest. But, since then I've noticed that he can't always keep his eyes off me. When I'm in a bathing suit or tight shorts or something, he'll always look, and then get all guilty and turn red and immediately start paying complete attention to Zoey.

It's kind of fun to watch. One harmless little kiss, but for him it's this big moral dilemma. That's Jake. The kind of guy who thinks he's committed a felony just because he likes to look at a pretty girl.

Faithful, honest, straight-arrow Jake.
You can read him like a book, and
you always know just where he
stands.

Kind of naive, even a little
ridiculous. But then again, after a
Lucas and a Benjamin, there are
times when you want a Jake.

Five

As Zoey was signing the letter, Claire was riding her bike the eight blocks from her house to Jake's. She stuck to the shore along the rocks, going past the dock and along the beach before turning into the steep driveway. It was too steep to ride her bike without getting hot and sweaty, so she leaned it against the McRoyans' mailbox and walked the rest of the way to the house.

She knocked at the front door and stood there on the porch, swatting away the flies that buzzed around the porch light. There was no answer, and when Claire looked, she noticed that there were no lights on inside.

She walked around the house, following the path past the garbage cans to the lower level where Jake's basement room opened onto the patio. Light spilled from his room.

"Claire?"

Nina's voice. She had come from the other direction, appearing through the bushes.

"What are you doing here?" Claire asked.

Nina grabbed her and pulled her away, out

of the pool of light from Jake's room. "What am *I* doing here? What are *you* doing here?"

"I'm stopping by to see Jake," Claire said calmly.

"You're stopping by to see Jake," Nina echoed incredulously. "Since when do you stop by to see Jake?"

"Since he asked for my history notes."

"Puh-leeze."

"You know, I don't have to check with you before I stop off and see a friend," Claire said icily. "But since you've poked your nose into *my* business, how about if you tell me why you're here?"

"Just passing by," Nina said.

But Claire noticed a white envelope stuck in the waistband of her sister's shorts. "What's that?"

"Nothing," Nina said instantly.

Claire laughed. Nina never had learned the knack of lying very well. "Okay, you don't have to tell me. But I'll bet it's something from Zoey."

Nina's eyes flared in unwilling acknowledgment.

"What, some mushy letter? Is she apologizing for making him look pathetic in front of the whole student body?"

"Does Benjamin know you're *visiting* Jake in his bedroom at night?" Nina asked sharply.

"I don't think so," Claire said.

"I bet he would be a little suspicious if he did," Nina said.

Claire made a wry smile. "Benjamin is always suspicious of one thing or another." She started to walk away, but Nina held her back.

"Claire, this is pretty sleazy, don't you think? Even for you. I mean, I don't even know if Zoey and Jake have officially broken up yet. And I know you haven't officially broken up with Benjamin."

"I'm just stopping by to give Jake my history notes," Claire said flatly. "Besides, Nina, I know how happy you'd be if I did break up with Benjamin, so don't try throwing that in my face."

"What are you talking about?" Nina demanded, a little too shrilly.

"Give me a break. Benjamin's the one who's blind, I'm not. I know you're all hot for him." She walked away, relieved that Nina said nothing further to stop her.

Well, that had been a piece of unfortunate luck. Nina was sure to tell Zoey, and she might even work up the nerve to tell Benjamin.

On the other hand, so what? These were minor secrets, in the grand scheme of things. As long as she could keep the real secret from all of them, everything would be all right.

Jake sat on his bed, staring at a dusty cardboard box, and took a long swallow from the beer. It was lukewarm, from one of the cases his dad kept in a

76

corner of the unfinished rec room for times when he had a bunch of people over for a barbecue.

Two empties lay crumpled in his trash basket. A third empty lay on its side on the floor.

He took the lid from the cardboard box and sneezed at the dust that rose from it. The box was marked JAKE'S JUNK in black Magic Marker. He turned it over, spilling the contents onto his comforter. A Red Sox pennant, from the time Wade and he drove all the way down to Boston to watch a game, just the two of them. Come to think of it, that had been the first time he'd ever had a whole beer. Wade had used his fake ID to buy them some. By the end of the game, it was Jake who'd had to drive all the way home, even though he was just fifteen and didn't have so much as a learner's permit.

Great day. The only time he'd gone to a ball game with Wade. Great day.

He drank some more of his beer, ignoring the sour taste, and opened a scrapbook. Newspaper clippings of Wade when he was the star fullback on the Weymouth High football team. A photo of the whole team together, Wade right at the front, looking cocky, as always. A ticket from Wade's junior prom. He was dead before his senior prom.

And the newspaper article about the accident, a sort of dividing line in the scrapbook. Before that article, most of the stuff was Wade's.

After, it turned to pictures of Jake himself, standing with the whole team and looking cocky.

A ticket from his own junior prom. He had taken Zoey, of course.

He finished the fourth beer and fumbled on the floor for the next one, cracked it open, and grimaced as he swallowed.

Zoey, of course.

He didn't dance very well, couldn't seem to keep track of the rhythm, and anyway he looked like a big trained bear wearing a suit or tuxedo, but Zoey had never minded.

Well, maybe she had. Maybe that was it. Maybe she was tired of dancing with a big trained bear who couldn't keep the beat. Maybe that was it. Maybe.

There was the picture of them together in front of a snowman they'd made in the circle. They were both wrapped in parkas and hats and laughing out clouds of steam.

And there they were on Town Beach, the ferry in the background. He was lifting her up, holding her in his arms, and she was smiling and laughing. Of course, Ninny had taken the picture, so most of his head had been cut off.

He closed the book and rocked forward, not caring that tears were rolling down his cheeks. He couldn't look at any more pictures. He wasn't drunk enough yet to think about her. He might never be drunk enough.

It took several seconds for him to realize that someone was tapping at his sliding glass door.

Zoey. Only Zoey came this way, straight to the sliding glass door.

He got up and forced himself to walk slowly to the door. If she thought she could just come and apologize and right away he'd take her back . . . well, she should think again. He wasn't going to let her off the hook that easily.

He wiped his face and slid open the door, forming a cold, forbidding expression on his face.

"Hi, Jake."

He stared, wondering if the beer was distorting his vision. "Claire?" he said at last.

"Yes," she said. "I'm sorry I'm not Zoey."

"I'm not," he said.

"Can I come in? I knocked upstairs at the front door, but—"

"My folks and my sister are over in Weymouth at some movie."

Claire glanced at the pile of mementos on his bed. "I don't want to interrupt you if you're busy," she said.

"Just junk," Jake said. He swept it back into the box and dropped the box onto the floor. He looked around uncertainly. The only chair he had was over by his desk. But Claire solved the problem by sitting at the end of his bed. He sat at the head, crossing his legs.

"I just mostly stopped by to tell you how sorry I am about you and Zoey," Claire said.

Jake nodded. It was safer than trying to speak on the subject of Zoey. He found the last beer of the six-pack and held it out for her.

"No, thanks. I haven't been interested much in drinking since . . . you know, since the accident."

"Well, I never drink and drive," Jake said. "I'm not Lucas." The name made him crumple the can in his hand. Some of the beer spurted out of the top and he drank it before it could stain the bed.

"No, you're definitely not Lucas," Claire said.

He looked at her sharply.

Claire smiled. "I mean, you know how I feel about Lucas. I can't understand why his father hasn't gotten rid of him yet." She leaned closer and put her hand on his. "Are you okay?"

He took a deep breath and let it out slowly, trying to still the quaver in his voice. "Yeah, I'm fine. It was just kind of a surprise, was all."

He fell silent, slipping back down into darkness, memories of Zoey, always laughing or smiling. That's how he thought of her. Always smiling, always so small in his arms.

"It's tough," Claire said, interrupting his thoughts.

"I'm sorry, what?"

"I said, it's tough. Losing a girlfriend. Or a boyfriend," she added with a wry smile. "I mean, I've lost a few of those over the years. Remember that guy Rick I used to go out with in eighth grade?"

"Yeah. Whatever happened to old Rick? What happens to old boyfriends when their girlfriends dump them?"

"He started going out with Courtney Howard. They've been together ever since."

Jake smiled ruefully. "So what you're telling me is don't worry, there are other girls?"

"I thought I was being more subtle than that," Claire said.

Jake smiled, but the smile couldn't last. His face fell, and Claire's eyes grew sad and sympathetic. She moved closer, sitting beside him, and put her arm around his shoulders.

"It's okay if you want to be sad, Jake," she said softly. "I won't like you any less if you cry. And I would never tell anyone. I'm good at keeping secrets."

Jake let her pull his head against her shoulder, and his tears did run down onto the white cotton of her blouse.

For a long time they lay that way, silent. Jake felt waves of bitterness, waves of anger, followed in turn by terrible sadness, loneliness.

Except that in his loneliness he felt Claire's warmth beside him. Felt her arm around him.

Even, to his embarrassment, felt the soft swell of her breasts.

Soon the tears dried up. *That's enough,* he told himself. *Enough tears for Zoey.* Right now Zoey was probably in Lucas's arms, kissing that creep. And he doubted very much that she was even sparing a moment's thought for him.

Strange what you learned about people. He would never have guessed that Zoey could be so cold-blooded.

And he would never have guessed that Claire could be so sympathetic.

"Thanks for coming over," he said, looking up into her dark eyes. The first words spoken in a long time.

"Anytime, Jake," she whispered.

Her mouth was so close to his that he could feel the words. So sweet to hear his name from her lips. So nice to be this close, to know that he wasn't really all alone.

Her lips were different from Zoey's. Fuller, softer, yet more forceful. It was she who kissed him, she who parted his lips with hers.

They had kissed once before, a long time ago, it seemed. Back then, he had been overwhelmed by feelings of guilt. Now it was as if all the life that had drained out of him came rushing back. And guilt wasn't even a memory.

Six

Aisha had left Zoey's house soon after Nina had gone to deliver the letter. She had fully intended to walk on up the hill and go home. But Zoey had put her in a bad mood. It was hard to be exposed at close range to all that weeping and sadness and regret without having it affect you at least a little. Frankly, Aisha resented it just a bit. Emotional people were always like that, always dumping their problems on you.

And it wasn't like anyone with half a brain couldn't see it coming. She'd told Zoey that getting involved with Lucas would lead to trouble. Why Zoey would decide to trade a nice guy like Jake for Lucas was totally beyond her. Lucas had been in one kind of trouble or another even before he decided to drive drunk, plow a car into a tree, and kill one of his few friends.

As she walked down from Zoey's toward the beach, Aisha passed Jake's house. Nina was probably still there, delivering Zoey's letter and waiting for Jake's reply. She considered waiting to see if Nina came out, but decided against it.

It would just mean more of the same. More *then he said, then I said*.

The night was cool but not cold, with wispy clouds concealing, then revealing stars, one moment hiding the moon and plunging the road into darkness, the next moment letting the moon shine bright and turn the road silver. The surf to her right broke on the beach with comforting regularity, a crash followed by the rattle of small stones being sucked into the undertow, a lull, then a new crash.

Across the water Weymouth was going to sleep. Most of the office buildings were dark, except for a few scattered lights where cleaning crews were at work.

To her left, many of the buildings she passed were dark. The tourist season was officially over now that Labor Day was past, and the big Victorian bed-and-breakfasts were mostly empty. Aisha herself lived with her parents and brother in an inn up on the ridge, and they had only a few reservations for the next month or so, and none past October.

Only one car had passed as Aisha walked along, rattling and belching as most island cars did. The roads were never exactly busy, even in July. It was expensive to bring cars over on the ferry, and there wasn't really anywhere to go that couldn't be easily reached on foot. And with a crime rate that was in essence zero, the island was infinitely safer than Boston, her childhood home.

She heard the whir of the bicycle just seconds before it blew past.

The rider applied his brakes and stopped twenty yards down the road and waited, straddling the bike and leaning on the handlebars.

"Christopher, tell me that isn't you," Aisha said wearily.

"I don't know, Aisha, I hate to start lying this early in our relationship."

"What do you do, follow me? I mean, every time I turn around . . ." She came up even with him and kept walking. "And don't tell me it's fate."

He rode slowly, keeping pace beside her. He was tall, just around six feet, and muscular in a wiry way. Walking or riding he always gave the impression that he was leaning forward, as if he were being propelled, or as if there were something he had to see first, before anyone else could pass him.

"I think it's just that we're on a small island together," Christopher said. "We're bound to run into each other. It's the law of probabilities." He caught her eye and smiled. "I would never say it's fate. I know how you feel about fate. You don't like anything you don't control."

Aisha started to object, but when she thought it over, she had to admit Christopher was right. "It's not so much that I want to control everything, it's just that I don't want to be controlled. Not by fate, not by some guy, not by school or parents or hormones or emotions. I make my own decisions." She nodded in satisfaction. That had sounded just right.

"Wow," Christopher said. "Sometimes your smugness absolutely amazes me. Takes my breath away. No one is that much in control. It doesn't work that way."

"It doesn't work any other way," Aisha said. "I just spent the evening with a certain friend who shall remain nameless, who doesn't even *try* to control herself. And she's been weeping and wailing since lunchtime today and will probably be weeping and wailing by lunch tomorrow. Plus, thanks to her, certain other people, who shall also remain nameless, are completely humiliated and depressed. Why? Because she believes in true romance, in true emotion, and she doesn't stop and ask herself, *Hmm, let's think this over and see where it's all likely to lead.* Even though certain of her friends, namely me, told her so all along."

Christopher laughed. "So the whole evening you've been sitting there with Zoey—who shall remain nameless—and having to resist the urge to jump around yelling *I told you so, I told you so.*" His broad smile was just visible in the moon's glow. "That must have been very, very hard for you."

"It was hell," Aisha admitted, laughing good-naturedly.

Christopher stopped. "I live right there." He nodded toward a sprawling Victorian with a tall turret on one end topped by a cone roof that gave it the air of a medieval castle.

"I've noticed the place before," Aisha said. "Cool turret."

"I have the top room in it," Christopher said. "It's small, but the landlady rents it to me cheap since I help out as the handyman."

"One of your ninety-four jobs."

"Just five jobs at the moment. I still cook at Zoey's folks' restaurant, but I'm getting fewer hours now that the season's over. The newspaper-delivery thing I still have, plus equipment manager and part-time soccer coach at your school, and the landscaping business. Still, if you add it all up, I'm only working about fifty hours a week. I'd like to do more, but jobs are scarce."

"Of course they're scarce," Aisha said. "You have them all."

"A man's got to eat and pay his rent. Not to mention saving for college. You want to come upstairs and see my palatial apartment?"

Aisha made a point of looking at her watch.

"Five minutes," Christopher said.

He parked his bike and led her inside a somewhat shabby foyer and up a set of stairs that creaked with every step. "My landlady usually rents out five different rooms," Christopher said as they climbed, "but right now there are only two other people staying here aside from her, so there's no one else on my floor."

They reached the top of the stairs and Christopher showed the way to his door, opening it onto an octagonal room with tall paned windows on three sides and a smaller window that opened onto the pitched roof. A single bed, neatly made, stuck out from one wall, and a desk was positioned by a window, giving him an excellent view of the beach and the waves during the day. Now it revealed a postcard-perfect view of Weymouth by night.

On one wall he had nailed up a dry marker board, where his work schedule was laid out on a red, blue, and green grid.

Instead of a closet, an iron pipe was suspended from the ceiling. On it hung white coats for cooking, overalls for landscaping, and bike shorts and rugby shirts for his work at the school. The room showed very little in the way of personal touches—no posters, no pictures, no mementos.

"It's very neat," Aisha said.

"It's a place to sleep," Christopher said.

"No pictures of your family or anything?" Aisha asked.

Christopher's face grew somber. "I like it uncluttered," he said flatly. Then he softened a little.

"I don't get along all that well with my family."

"Who does?" Aisha joked.

"No, I mean we don't really communicate anymore. I haven't seen them or spoken to them since I graduated four months ago and came up here."

Aisha realized she was on touchy ground. This was the first time she'd ever seen Christopher seem uncomfortable or unsure of himself. "I guess you'd like me to drop it, huh?"

Christopher shrugged. "It's no big deal. We're just the typical screwed-up inner-city family. No father. My mom's on welfare. She was on crack for a year, but she got off that and now she just drinks. My older sister's living with a creep who takes all her money." He made a derisive noise. "Not much like your family, Aisha."

Aisha was stunned. It seemed impossible that this arrogant, confident, often annoying guy should come from a background like that.

She had always been comfortably middle class. Not that her parents didn't sometimes have money problems. In fact, they acted like they'd go broke if Aisha bought one too many outfits or failed to finish the food on her plate.

"How did you end up here in Maine, on Chatham Island?" Aisha asked, looking at him with renewed curiosity.

"Baltimore's very hot in the summer,"

Christopher said wryly. "I decided if I was getting out of Baltimore, I was going to head north and at least stay cool."

"Wait till you check out February. You may change your mind. Kids here compete to come up with new descriptions for the cold. Last year's most popular entry was *icicle enema*. And it's not an exaggeration." She tilted her head and stared at him thoughtfully.

"What?"

"I just didn't picture you coming out of the projects."

"Coming *out*. Staying out. Never going back," he said with quiet conviction. "I learned two things growing up there. One, life isn't fair. Some people are born with everything, others are born with nothing and it just gets worse— bad neighborhoods, bad schools, bad teachers, bad parents or no parents at all. Guns and drugs and violence all around. It's like some huge conspiracy to keep you from staying alive, let alone making anything of yourself. Most people fail. Most people don't have a chance."

Aisha looked at him thoughtfully. "And the second thing you learned?" she asked softly.

"I learned that I'm not *most people*," he said, focusing an intense gaze on her. "I don't care how impossible it is to succeed. I like it that way. Impossible doesn't bother me. It's going to take more than that."

"I did sort of notice that you are persistent," Aisha said dryly.

"I make a point of getting what I want," he said, stepping closer.

"But there are *some* things even you can't get."

Christopher broke into a grin. "You could just give in now and save us both a lot of trouble."

"Oh, no, I don't think so, Christopher," Aisha said. "Besides, you just said you like it hard. And I have to get home." She turned and headed for the door.

"You do know we're going to keep running into each other," Christopher said.

"It can't be totally avoided," Aisha said.

"Tomorrow night is bargain night at the movies," Christopher said casually. "Two-dollar tickets. Do you ever go?"

"Occasionally," Aisha admitted.

"Then we might accidentally run into each other there, too."

Aisha hesitated, her hand on the doorknob. It wasn't like a commitment. It wasn't like he was asking her out on a date. Not really. He was just pointing out the obvious. It was a small island and a small world and people sometimes ran into each other. "Like I said, it can't be totally avoided."

"Hello, Passmore residence."

"Hi, it's me."

"Nina? What are you doing calling? Where are you? I thought you were coming straight back here after you gave Jake my letter."

"Well, it is kind of late."

"So what did he say?"

"Um, nothing."

"What do you mean, nothing?"

"I mean, I didn't give him the letter."

"Nina! You said you'd do it."

"I tried, only . . ."

"He wasn't there?"

"Um . . . I'm not sure if he was there."

"Look, Nina, just tell me whatever it is you're trying so hard not to tell me."

"I can't, Zoey. It will be like tattling or something. I mean, you're my best friend and all, but jeez, I can't be spying for you."

"Spying on who?"

"Anyone. It's not really up to me to tell you certain things. It's up to certain people to tell you certain things. I only called because I had to tell you that I couldn't deliver the letter. Otherwise I wouldn't have called at all."

"Nina. Just tell me why you didn't give Jake the letter."

"Zoey—"

"You said you don't know if he was home or not, which means whatever your reason is, it couldn't be because he wasn't home. Right?"

"Zoey—"

"Was someone else there? Is that it?"

"I have to go now."

"Who was it? It wasn't Benjamin; he's here. Obviously it wasn't me or you or Aisha because she left after you did. Are you telling me Claire was there?"

"I haven't said anything, I want the record to be clear on that. I never said—"

"There is no record, Nina. Claire was with him. Claire was over at Jake's house at night. That's it, isn't it? Well, it didn't take her long, did it?"

"She was probably just bringing him some homework or something."

"Right. Homework. That bitch, if she's going behind my brother's back, I'll kill her. That would really tear Benjamin apart, and the least she could do is break up with him first."

"You mean like you told Jake before you started letting Lucas stick his tongue down your throat?"

"Oh."

"Sorry, that was rotten. I shouldn't have said that, but I feel bad I told you about Jake and Claire. I don't handle guilt well. I lash out."

"No, I deserved it, Nina. It's true."

"Yeah, but best friends aren't supposed to tell you the truth about yourself."

"Do you think it was . . . I mean, do you think Jake and Claire . . ."

93

"I didn't stay and watch, Zoey. But she's still not home."

"Oh. Oh, God. I guess I'm getting a taste of my own medicine. It seems strange to think of Jake with some other girl. Jake with Claire. I guess it's not really any of my business, is it?"

"Are you going to tell Benjamin?"

"I don't think so. I mean, I don't want to look like I'm spying around."

"You mean like me."

"Sorry, Nina. I seem to be turning into a major hypocrite."

"Well, don't hang yourself, Zoey. You had to fall off your pedestal of perfection sooner or later. It's kind of reassuring, actually, seeing you screwing up your life for once."

"Thanks."

"I didn't think you were capable of causing this much trouble all by yourself."

"Thanks."

"I mean, it's like you're a one-woman disaster, with ripples of hostility and jealousy and distrust—"

"Okay, Nina, enough."

"—engulfing Jake and Benjamin and Claire and even me and Eesh."

"I'm so glad you called, Nina."

"Just remember, I never told you anything."

"I'll remember. At least now I'm not feeling so much pity for Jake."

"Funny, I'm feeling more. Poor *Joke*, being comforted by Claire."

"I wonder if he kissed her?"

"I doubt it, Zoey. Besides, you don't care, right?"

"Right."

"Okay, see you tomorrow."

"Bye, Nina."

Claire

12:42 a.m. Fifty-seven degrees.
Wind at eight knots, gusting to twelve,
out of the southwest. Barometer stable.
The front that came through yesterday
just dropped a little light rain and
moved on. Tonight we have wispy
clouds and a warm evening.

I went over to Jake's house tonight
to see if he was okay. He was pretty
depressed over Zoey, naturally. But
by the time I left, I think he was
feeling better.

We made out for a while. He's
very different from Benjamin. Like

he's not quite as in control, and cool as Benjamin always is. It's funny, because Benjamin's only a year older than Jake, but in some ways he seems so much older. I don't think Benjamin would ever have let himself cry in front of me, or seem so out front about the way he feels. Benjamin's always a mystery, which is exactly what he says about me. Jake is different.

I really didn't expect to make out with Jake, not that I wasn't interested. But it happened so naturally. He was so sad over Zoey and also, I think, from remembering Wade.

I guess I'm partly responsible for

what happened to Wade. I don't think I'm completely responsible because all three of us, Lucas and Wade and I, were drunk. Any one of us could have been driving.

Still, I guess I am at least partly responsible. So I think I did the right thing taking Jake's mind off at least some of his trouble.

I'll have to tell Benjamin soon. I don't want to do to him what Zoey did to Jake. I owe him a straightforward explanation.

Besides, Nina is incapable of keeping a secret, so it's bound to come out before long.

I've decided. I'll tell Benjamin

it's over. Tomorrow, on the ferry, before he can find out some other way.

The one thing I can be sure of is that he won't be as devastated as Jake was.

It was strange with Jake. I was strange with Jake. I felt different. Like at that moment he was really glad I was there. Like he needed me. That's exactly what it was, I felt like Jake needed me.

Benjamin never needs anyone but Benjamin.

Seven

Claire held her books close to her chest like a shield and climbed the ramp onto the morning ferry. Lucas, Zoey, and Nina were already up on the top deck, standing at the back of the boat. Zoey looked down, refusing to meet Claire's eyes.

Turning, Claire could just see Jake trotting across the parking lot, followed closely by Aisha. Benjamin was seated toward the bow, alone.

Now would be the time, Claire told herself. Now, before Jake got on board.

She walked purposefully up to Benjamin, feeling at once determined and nervous. The nervousness bothered her. She had blown off guys before. Never quite this way, and never someone she'd been with as long as she'd been with Benjamin. But still, that was no reason for feeling almost sick.

She sat down on the bench beside Benjamin. "Hi, Benjamin," she said.

"Claire," he said in his neutral voice.

She sat there for a moment, trying to remember all the things she had memorized to say. Something about how people could change, and that was good, not bad. Something about how it wasn't like Benjamin would have a hard time finding another girl to go out with. And something else about how neither of them had ever said this was forever.

"Shouldn't you be sitting with Jake?" Benjamin asked.

Claire's mouth dropped open. "What . . . what do you mean?"

He laughed scornfully. "Come on, Claire, you can do better than that stuttering act. I've known for a long time that you were setting your sights on Jake."

"Nina told you?"

"No. Nina told Zoey, and Zoey's my sister. She loves me." He said the last words with a tinge of bitterness.

"Look, Benjamin," Claire said, flustered, "no one ever said it was going to last forever between us."

"That's what you practiced up to say?" Benjamin demanded, sending her a wry, deprecating look. "What else? We'll always be good friends? Come on, Claire. I'm disappointed in you. I expected some style."

"Sorry I didn't write better material. Maybe if I'd opened with a few jokes—"

"Jake will be an interesting change for you, Claire. You've always needed to find a guy you could feel superior to." He smiled sadly. "That's what you thought you were getting with me."

"That's not true," Claire said.

"Sure it is. You're an isolated, lonely, superior person, Claire. You sit up there on your widow's walk and watch the clouds overhead and the little people down below. And they have to be below you, that's the important thing, because you can't tolerate an equal for long."

Claire realized her hands had formed fists. He was hurting her deliberately. He knew none of what he said was true, he was just saying it to get back at her for leaving him. "I think you're talking about yourself, Benjamin. You're the one who is isolated and . . . what was it? Lonely? Superior?"

Benjamin nodded. "Yeah, that's it. And it's why, sooner or later, you'll get bored with Jake and come back to me. Because we are so much alike, Claire, you and me."

Claire gathered her books and stood up. "You know, I was feeling bad about breaking up with you, but now I feel better. I'm glad I'm breaking up with you. You're a jerk, Benjamin. You are arrogant beyond belief."

Benjamin nodded. "Enjoy life with Jake, for as long as it lasts."

"It will last as long as I want it to," Claire

snapped. "Just like our relationship."

"Or until Jake learns the truth."

Claire froze. "What are you talking about now?" she asked, loading her voice with weary disinterest.

"It's small island, Claire. Too small for big secrets to be hidden for long."

"You think anyone will believe you if you go around saying I—" She glanced around and dropped her voice to a whisper. "You think you can go around telling people I'm responsible for the accident? No one's going to believe you. They'll just think you're trying to hurt me for dumping you."

"I would never tell," Benjamin said sincerely.

"There's nothing *to* tell," Claire snapped.

"Of course there is, Claire. You really think you can lie to me? I know you've remembered. Just a week ago the only people who knew the truth for sure were Lucas, and, I believe, your father."

Claire gasped involuntarily.

"In one week we've gone from two people knowing to four. Your father won't tell, and neither will I, because as strange as it feels to admit this, Claire, I really do love you. But what about Lucas? How long will he keep your secret?"

Claire glanced sharply at Lucas, standing at the far end of the boat, laughing at something

103

Nina had said, his hand casually intertwined with Zoey's.

"You want my prediction?" Benjamin asked in a soft voice. "I think in the end you'll be the one to tell the truth."

"Me?" Claire asked incredulously. "If what you're saying *were* true, why would I do that?"

Benjamin shrugged and smiled his wry half smile. "Because in the end, as self-serving and ruthless as you are, Claire, when the line is drawn between right and wrong, I think you'll do the right thing."

"You okay?" Zoey asked her brother, sitting down beside him.

"Yeah," Benjamin said. His head was bowed forward. "It was okay. At least I deprived her of the pleasure of dumping me. Thanks to you."

"I don't think even Claire would have gotten much pleasure out of that," Zoey said. "I'm just starting to realize how painful it can be."

Claire and Jake had gone below to the lower deck, out of sight, but not out of Zoey's imagination. It bothered her, thinking of them together, thinking that Jake was probably comparing her to Claire. Claire was beautiful in a dark, sultry way that lots of guys seemed to like. She had great, long silky black hair and a disgustingly perfect body. Probably by now Jake was glad that Zoey was out of his life.

"Anyway, it's over," Benjamin said. "For now at least."

"You don't think it will last between Claire and Jake?" Zoey asked.

Benjamin grinned. "Two weeks." He stuck out his hand.

Zoey shook his hand. "I say six weeks, for ten bucks."

"Make it five bucks," Benjamin said. "I already bet a guy at school five bucks that you and Lucas wouldn't last three months."

Zoey punched her brother in the arm.

"Oh, fine, beat up on the poor, helpless blind guy," Benjamin said.

"Helpless, right," Zoey said. "Look, you want to go to a movie tonight? We could pick something with a good sound track."

"A movie on a Tuesday?"

Zoey sighed. "It's a long story. Aisha wants to go because she kind of told Christopher she would, only, if she shows up alone, it will look like she's going on a date with him. If there's a bunch of us, Aisha can act like it was just a coincidence. So Lucas and I are going, too."

"I won't even try to make sense out of that. But I don't think I should go. I'd be the fifth wheel, no date."

"Nina's coming, too," Zoey said.

"Nina's not exactly a date," Benjamin said. "But sure, why not?"

"See, that's perfect, because then you and Nina won't really be on a date so Aisha can say that she and Christopher weren't really on a date, they were just like you and Nina."

"Well, as long as it all makes sense to you."

"I've decided that where romance is concerned, nothing ever makes sense," Zoey said a little wistfully.

Eight

1. The major Axis powers in World War II were
   - a. Germany, Japan, and France
   - b. Japan, Russia, and England
   - c. Germany, Japan, and Italy
   - d. All of the above

Nina chewed her number-two pencil and looked up at the ceiling. All of the above? Possibly. But all six of them couldn't be *major* Axis powers, that seemed obvious. So, it wasn't *d*. That left three possibilities.

Benjamin would know. He'd know right off the top of his head. Of course, he was a senior, and she was only a junior. Maybe that was the problem. Maybe he just didn't want to date a junior. So she'd have to try to be extra sophisticated tonight at the movie. No dumb jokes, just the occasional witty observation. Fortunately, with Benjamin you didn't have to worry how you were dressed because there'd be no time to get back to the island and change.

But you did have to worry how you smelled.

Extra-long shower in gym.

Axis was the bad guys, so it couldn't be England, right? Weren't they the good guys usually? Except during the Revolution. And the War of 1812.

Wait a minute. Germany was definitely involved, so that eliminated *b*, anyway. So, it was down to *a* and *c*. Either France or Italy was the third bad guy. France or Italy.

Would they be able to sit together? Zoey was sure to sit next to Lucas, but maybe Aisha wouldn't want to actually sit next to Christopher. Aisha might sit on one end, then Zoey and Lucas, then . . . either Christopher or Benjamin. If Nina got between the two of them, she was okay. But what if Christopher was on the far end and she ended up the last person, with Benjamin too far away?

France or Italy. Mussolini! Yes, Mussolini! It was all coming back now. Mussolini was one of the bad guys, and that was definitely an Italian name.

She filled the little circle beside *c*.

Zoey, Fourth Period

"In the second book in the series the author creates a hurricane that we first see as a distant threat, far offshore from our mythical small beach town. At first we don't think it will be important, but because the author keeps coming back to it, reminding us that it is out there waiting, she . . . she does what? Um, Zoey?"

"Excuse me?"

"What do we call this technique?" the teacher asked. "Daydreaming again, Ms. Passmore? We call this foreshadowing. The author is foreshadowing."

Foreshadowing.

Zoey wrote in her notebook. Of course.

Foreshadowing. Like when you let the reader know that something is probably going to happen later in the book and that way the reader is anticipating it.

Like when one of your friends tells you you'd better be honest and let your old boyfriend know that you're breaking up. That would be foreshadowing. Or when you've noticed some girl who is always making eyes at your old boyfriend and when you do finally break up she rushes in to grab him without even waiting a day. That whole thing had been

109

foreshadowed, but Zoey was still surprised. Right now Jake and Claire were whispering to each other. They had changed seats so they could sit side by side. What did that foreshadow?

"It was foreshadowing by use of a metaphor. Claire? Metaphor, if you can stop whispering long enough to answer?"

"Metaphor is when you use one thing to describe another. Like, um, like the fog was a blanket, or the clouds marched with military precision."

She's just showing off for Jake.

Suddenly Claire cares about English.

Zoey wrote in her notebook.

"And what is the metaphor in this book, and what does it foreshadow?"

Great, Zoey thought, *I know the answer to that question, but no, the teacher has to jump me when I'm thinking about something else.*

Claire thought for a moment. "Well, I think the hurricane is a metaphor for the heroine's own passion. It's a metaphor for sexual desire. At first it was just out there, harmless, but as it came inexorably closer it became more powerful, more overwhelming, more dangerous, until the heroine was caught up and swept away by it."

Zoey rolled her eyes. Half the guys in the room were now sitting there with their tongues hanging out. Including Jake. And it wasn't even the right answer. The metaphor in the book had nothing to do with sex.

"Absolutely correct," the teacher said.

Aisha, Fifth Period

"The square root of two x plus zy over p prime?" Aisha said.

"Correct, except that you have to remember your parentheses," the teacher said.

Aisha winced, then shook her head good-naturedly. "Of course. I meant to say that."

"It is important to be precise."

Aisha nodded in complete agreement. It was absolutely important to be precise. Leave out a variable or misplace a parentheses and the whole meaning of the equation would change.

"Has anyone solved this yet for x?" the teacher asked.

Aisha had, but she didn't want to be a show-off. When she saw that Louis Goldman was getting ready to raise his hand, though, hers shot up quickly. No one was a bigger show-off than Louis, and she couldn't let him sit there and gloat. Not after she'd forgotten her parentheses.

She should never have worn this top. It was cut too low. Not slutty low, just low enough that

Christopher would probably think she'd worn it for him.

"Aisha?"

"*X* equals negative three."

The teacher winked. "I see you remembered the parentheses when you solved the equation. Correct. *X* equals negative three."

Of course it did, Aisha thought. All around her kids wrinkled their foreheads and went back to their notebooks. Obviously a lot of them had come up with the wrong answer, which was hard to understand. How could you look at a simple equation and not understand it? It was so logical.

If everything in the world were so logical, life would be . . . well, it would be logical. One plus one equals two. It never equals three. That was how everything should be.

Christopher was bound to think it was a date. Which meant he would probably try to put his arm around her. What should she do? She didn't want to make a big scene, but by the same token she didn't want anyone to misunderstand.

"Now, let's talk about parabolas," the teacher said.

Parabolas, good. She'd read ahead into this section, and it was really interesting stuff. In fact, she'd much rather be spending her evening understanding parabolas than going to a movie with Christopher.

No, not *with* Christopher. *Near* Christopher. Maybe not even so near. They didn't even have to sit together. She could sit between Zoey and Nina. Or she could sit between Benjamin and Zoey, if Benjamin sat by his sister. Or . . .

Wait a minute. This could be an equation. Zoey would be z, Nina n, Benjamin b . . . It was a lot of variables, but with a little work she could have a strategy for every possible arrangement of points—or people—along a straight line, which was to say, a row of seats.

Nina, Sixth Period

Okay, Lucas goes down the aisle first, then Zoey. That leaves me, Benjamin, Aisha, and Christopher. So I say something funny like, Hey, all you couples should be together and leave us single people to ourselves. Of course, then Aisha gives me a death look, but she's trapped, right? She has to go, either her first or Christopher first, which means either way Benjamin and I end up sitting together.

What if it's Aisha first? Then naturally Christopher would go next, followed, hopefully, by Lucas and Zoey. Unless Benjamin jumps in there and ends up between Christopher and either Lucas or Zoey.

"—I'm sorry, would you repeat the question?" Nina snapped back just before the teacher came down the aisle, prepared to pull her famous rap-on-the-head wake-up.

"The question, which you would have heard the first time if you had been paying attention, Nina Geiger, was 'What do you call a verbal construction that involves a repetition of examples all making the same point?' And since I very much doubt that you know the—"

"That would be a tautology," Nina said.

The teacher's mouth hung open, and thirty heads turned to stare at Nina.

Nina grinned back. *Ha. Thought you had me there, didn't you?*

"Do you think you could offer an example?" the teacher asked poisonously.

"Yes, ma'am. Um, okay, like a funny example would be if I say that I love this class like a hungry baby loves his mother's nipple, like a . . . like a drunk loves a toilet with plenty of room to kneel, like a hooker loves a sailor on leave . . . Wait, one more—like a teenage guy loves his hand."

When the laughter died down, the teacher asked Nina if she knew the way to the principal's office. She did, and went off down the hall shaking her head.

Never should have gone for that fourth one, she chided herself. *I've always said three was the right number. When I tell this story to Benjamin tonight, I'll leave one out. After all, I'm going for sophisticated.*

"I'm not going to see a slasher movie," Zoey said firmly. "I don't see how people can find it entertaining to watch women being murdered. Sorry."

They stood in a little gaggle outside the multiplex at the Weymouth Mall. Night was falling as cars with their lights on cruised through the parking lot, trying for parking places near the entrance. The crowd outside was sparse. Tuesday was not a big movie night, at least not now that school was back in session.

"It isn't really a slasher movie, and besides, lots of people get killed, not *just* girls," Lucas countered without much conviction. "It's an action movie. It's what's-his-name, Jean Claude, um, Seagull or whatever. The karate guy."

"I don't like violent movies," Zoey said. Maybe it wasn't a major moral stand, Zoey thought, but she had decided after the last violent movie she'd seen, and the subsequent case of willies, that she was going to avoid similar stuff in the future.

"Me neither," Aisha agreed.

"Okay, there's seven other movies," Christopher pointed out.

"Six," Benjamin said. "Because I'm not sitting through another movie about animated characters who save the rain forest or whatever. Shrill, shrieking voices bitching about the environment and every now and then breaking into a bad, bad song. It makes my skin crawl."

"I agree with Benjamin," Nina said. "Crawling skin should be avoided."

"How about *My Sister's Boyfriend*?" Zoey suggested. "It's supposed to be hilarious."

"I heard it sucked," Nina said quickly. "I mean, who cares? A movie about some girl going out with her sister's boyfriend? I mean, so what, right?"

"Three down, five to go," Aisha noted, looking uncomfortable standing beside Christopher.

"The lawyer movie?" Benjamin suggested.

"I'll bet it won't be as good as the one with Tom Cruise," Aisha said.

"You know, he's really short," Lucas said. "About five one."

"And I heard he never takes a shower," Benjamin suggested.

"You guys are so pathetic," Zoey said, giving Lucas a playful shove.

"How about the Michael Keaton movie?" Aisha said. "I like Michael Keaton."

"I like him, too," Zoey agreed.

"I like him, but not when he was Batman," Lucas offered.

"I like Batman, but not when he was Michael Keaton," Nina said. Then she seemed to glance nervously at Benjamin and smiled only when he laughed. What was with Nina tonight? Zoey wondered. She seemed jumpy or something.

They bought tickets and munchies and paraded into the theater, arguing about the relative merits of Milk Duds versus Raisinettes. When they came to an aisle toward the middle of the mostly empty theater, Lucas led the way with Zoey. They went down six seats and sat. Then Zoey realized no one was following.

"You guys don't like these seats?" Zoey asked.

"They're fine. After you, Aisha," Nina said.

"Well, are you coming next?" Aisha asked.

"What do you care?" Nina asked suspiciously.

"I don't, I was just wondering. Because I'll go sit down, but, you know, uh, who would go next?"

Zoey exchanged a mystified look with Lucas. "Excuse me, but is this really that great a challenge?" she asked Nina and Aisha.

"Well, how about if I go sit down next?" Christopher said.

"Fine," Aisha said. "Then you can go, Nina."

"What, and you'll sit on the aisle?" Nina asked Aisha.

"Excuse me, but *I* have to sit on the aisle," Benjamin said. "I have a hard time navigating over people's feet."

"Let's see," Zoey said, "Benjamin's on the aisle, Christopher's next to me; by my count that leaves two seats and, oh, surprise! Two

117

of you. Or should I try to find my calculator?"

"After you, Eesh," Nina said, standing back.

"No, really, go ahead," Aisha said, stepping still farther back.

"Have those two finally lost their minds?" Zoey asked.

"Nah," Christopher said, contentedly munching his popcorn. "It's just Aisha doesn't want to sit next to me because then this would be a date."

"Oh," Zoey said. Of course. "Well, then, what's the matter with Nina?"

Christopher laughed. "I thought Nina was always like this."

"You have a point there," Zoey said.

"The movie is starting," Lucas said.

"Aisha," Christopher said, raising his voice a little. "It's not a date, all right? You have amnesty. I will not count this as a date. I won't even try to put my arm around you."

Aisha's eyes blazed, but she stomped down the aisle, plopping next to Christopher. "That wasn't the problem. The problem was Nina wouldn't make up her mind."

Nina promptly took the next seat and Benjamin fumbled for and found the aisle seat.

"I have an idea," Lucas said brightly. "Let's all change seats again."

*   *   *

LUCAS

This movie chews. Jeez, I thought it was supposed to be a comedy. My hand is numb. I've been holding Zoey's hand for forty minutes and now I can't feel my fingers. Plus, my hand is sweaty. I'd like to kiss her, but her brother is just a few seats away. I know he can't see, but still. Not to mention her friends. It would be like having an audience going, Oh, that was a good one, or worse yet, Ooh, bad lip noise. We give a thumbs-down, way down, for that kiss.

Zoey

It's so romantic, the way he's just happy to hold hands and doesn't have to try to feel me up like Jake always did. He's probably nervous with everyone here. Besides, the movie's so good, who wants to spend the whole time making out? Especially with Aisha sitting there, probably thinking what a backstabbing bitch I am making out with Lucas while Jake is probably home alone. Maybe I am a backstabbing bitch. Am I?

Christopher

HER THIGH IS TOUCHING MINE. SHE MUST BE AWARE OF IT, I MEAN, IT'S LIKE ALL I'M AWARE OF RIGHT NOW. SKIN TO SKIN. THANK GOD I WORE SHORTS. THANK GOD SHE WORE THAT TOP. THANK GOD THE AIR CONDITIONING IN HERE IS SO COLD. AFTERWARD, IF WE GO GET SOMETHING TO EAT, I HAVE TO REMEMBER TO SIT ACROSS FROM HER. SHE'S SO BEAUTIFUL. I'D

SELL MY RIGHT ARM TO HAVE HER. AS
LONG AS IT COULD BE REMOVED PAIN-
LESSLY. ALTHOUGH THAT MIGHT SCREW
UP WORKING. CAN'T COOK WITH ONE ARM.

Aisha

If I pull my leg away,
he'll think Aha! I got to her.
She got too excited, so she had
to pull away. If I just leave
it there, though, he might think
I like it. And I don't. I'll
bet he can't believe I'm not
paying more attention to him.
Mr. Ego. He probably figured
I'd be sitting here by now
playing kissy face. Although he
hasn't tried anything yet. And
the movie is half over. Is it
the Red Hots? Did they give
me bad breath?

Nina

Maybe I could just kill myself.
Maybe I could just wedge my head in
the seat and suffocate. He leans over,
we're in the dark, his lips actually
almost brush my ear, I can feel his
warm breath on my neck, and what
do I do? I inhale a piece of popcorn.
Very nice, very romantic. As he leans
close I suck popcorn and say HIΓΓΓΓΤΗ
HHGHAGH. He's probably getting
ready to say, I've just realized,
Nina, how much I like being with
you; you're so funny and yet sexy,
so sophisticated and yet playful,
unlike your sister, ice woman. And as
he's getting ready to whisper this in

my ear, I say HIKIKTH HHGHAGH, a sound that will make him associate the name Nina with the word mucus for the rest of his life.

Benjamin

Wow, I wonder if this movie's any better if you can see? Probably not. I miss Claire. When I went to a movie with Claire, I didn't have to worry if the movie was any good. It makes me sick how much I miss her. It makes me sick thinking of her with Jake. Not that I blame Jake. Everyone says she's beautiful, and after getting dumped by my sister, Jake probably feels like going out with Claire erases his humiliation. Plus she's probably kissing him the way she used to kiss me. Maybe I should learn from Jake. Maybe I should find some girl to date, at least until Claire and Jake break up. But who? There's really only one girl I know who . . . But I guess she's going out with Christopher. Damn, I miss Claire. I wonder what she's doing right now?

Nine

Claire sat beside Jake on the bench seat of his beat-up old pickup truck. A cassette was playing on the stereo as they drove at no more than five miles an hour, making their progress along the shoreline last. There was no traffic on the road, no one in a hurry, and even with the music playing Claire could hear the surf pounding, the crunch of loose sand and rocks under the truck's tires.

"What's this music?" Claire asked.

"Lyle Lovett. It's one of my dad's tapes, but I kind of like it."

Claire nodded. The songs struck her as melancholy, but then, maybe Jake was in a melancholy mood. They came to an intersection. The road going left led along the north shore of Big Bite Pond, the inlet that nearly cut Chatham Island in half, like a huge bite taken out of the middle of a croissant. Ahead, the road led out onto the Lip, a peninsula that was a favorite make-out location.

Jake hesitated.

"Let's drive out onto the Lip," Claire said. "I

like it out there. It's so isolated."

They drove the few hundred yards of gravel road and stopped at the dead end. On the left was the placid, glass-smooth pond; just to their right, the more agitated water of the sea itself. Across the inlet was the Lower Lip, home to a colony of puffins, part of the nature preserve. The spit of land they were standing on was so narrow that thirty steps would take them from pond to sea.

Claire climbed out of the truck and looked across at the puffins, who were hopping around the rocks, purring and croaking and from time to time yelling out what sounded like *Hey, Al!* The tide was going out, sucking water through the inlet, and in the sky towering thunderheads floated over Weymouth, sending occasional jagged bolts of lightning down to the city. Directly overhead, the sky was still clear, with darkness falling fast and stars winking into sight, saying brief hellos before the storm clouds could advance and hide them.

"Hi, remember me?"

Claire saw Jake standing a few feet away, hands in his pockets. She must have been lost in thought for longer than she realized.

"Sorry, I guess I was spacing."

Jake looked out at the storm. "You think that's coming this way?"

Claire nodded. "It will be here in about twenty minutes, I would guess. But it's an isolated storm cell, and the wind is veering west, so it may just miss us."

Jake smiled. "Everyone thinks it's strange the way you're so interested in the weather."

"Weather is great," Claire said. "It's what keeps one day from being just like the next. And it's a system of incredible complexity, all sorts of forces interacting so that warm water five thousand miles away in the Pacific and a strong breeze in Africa all have an effect on what happens here." She fell silent, watching the storm. "On the other hand, maybe I am just strange."

"Is that what you're going to do in college? Study weather?"

"Meteorology, climatology, hydrography. Yes. And then later, while I'm working on my doctorate, I'm going to try to get an assignment in Antarctica. Antarctica is the home office of strange, unknown weather patterns."

"Cold, isn't it?" Jake asked lightly.

"That's what I hear," Claire said. "Ninety below zero in some places during the winter. Plus hurricane-force winds."

"Sounds nice," Jake said dryly. "But I guess it must be good to have something you want to do and really care about."

"Don't you?" Claire asked, turning now to face him.

"I like football, and I'll probably make the

team in college, but you can't exactly count on making the NFL. It would be great, but you have to have some backup. You know, a *real* job."

"So what are you going to major in?"

He scrunched up his shoulders and made a face. "I have no idea. I thought about criminal justice. You know, become a cop."

She tilted her head and looked at him critically. "I could see you in the uniform."

"I can see you with ten layers of long johns and a fur hood and those big plastic boots, too," he said. "But I like you better this way."

Claire felt a wave of cooler air, a breeze pushed before the onrushing storm. "You just like me because you needed someone after Zoey hurt you."

Instantly she regretted her words. Jake's eyes showed a wounded look, like she'd slapped him. She would have to try and be a little gentler. Jake wasn't like Benjamin, who seemed to be encased in unscratchable armor. She had gotten into the habit of being blunt and provocative with Benjamin. It was hard to remember just how vulnerable this big, powerful-looking guy could be.

"Maybe that's partly true," Jake said softly. "I mean, I was pretty torn up . . . but that's not why I like you, not really."

Claire took his right hand in both of hers. "I didn't mean that quite the way it sounded."

127

"I always liked you, as a friend, at least," Jake said. "And I always thought you were sexy." He gave her a deliberately comic leer.

Claire searched her memory for the words Benjamin had snapped at her. "Then you don't think I'm isolated, lonely, and superior?"

"I don't know if you're lonely," Jake said. "Are you?"

"Not when I'm with you," Claire answered.

"Then you'll have to be with me as much as possible," Jake said.

Claire raised his hand to her lips and kissed the hard, rough fingers. She looked at his face as his lowered eyes looked down at her. *Is this real?* Claire asked herself. *Is what I feel for him right this minute real? How could it be, when it all happened so quickly?*

Had she secretly cared for him for months and years? She couldn't remember feeling that way.

Or was this just two people brought together by coincidence, both of them needing someone at the same moment?

Zoey had torn Jake's heart out. Benjamin had forced her to remember a truth she did not want to face. Were they just two drowning, desperate people clinging to whoever came along?

She felt his lips on hers. It was pleasurable, certainly. Different from Benjamin, different from her memories of Lucas. Certainly there was something wonderful in feeling Jake's powerful arms around her, pressing her to his hard chest, and his shoulders, hunched forward, completed the sense that he was engulfing her, surrounding her with protection.

Jake was hot where Benjamin was cool; straightforward where Benjamin was subtle; bigger, stronger, yet touchingly vulnerable, where Benjamin so often seemed at once frail in his blindness and yet somehow invulnerable.

There could not be a greater difference between the two of them. And she realized that she herself felt different here, with Jake, than she did with Benjamin. As if she were literally a different person with Jake.

A nicer person.

She broke away, feeling slightly annoyed for no reason. She glanced toward the mainland and saw that the storm was advancing fast across the channel, whipping up the water, turning the choppy waves white.

"Here it comes," she said.

"We'd better get back in the truck," he said.

She was about to say that she wanted to go home now. That she wanted to put on her poncho and sit up on her widow's walk alone where she could revel in the storm at close quarters. But she stopped herself. Jake wouldn't understand. He would think she was tired of him, bored, or somehow unhappy with his kisses.

It would hurt his feelings. And she couldn't do that to him.

They all took the nine-o'clock ferry, the *Titanic*, back from the mainland after the movie. It was the last homeward-bound ferry of the night, and missing it would mean being stranded on the mainland or having to pay the exorbitant cost for the water taxi. The *Titanic* was the ferry that carried cars and had a smaller covered space than the *Minnow*, but the rain drove them all inside, watching lightning strikes through steamed windows.

The rain had cleared away by the time they reached the island, leaving behind glistening cobblestones and a fresh, electric smell in the air.

They split up at the ferry landing, Nina heading north, Christopher heading south along Leeward Drive, leaving Aisha looking slightly annoyed. Lucas and Benjamin, Aisha and Zoey walked in a group as far as Camden before Aisha went on ahead, making the tiring climb up the winding road to her parents' inn on the ridge.

Benjamin, always diplomatic, went alone into the house, leaving Lucas with Zoey in her front yard, the first privacy they'd had that evening.

"Well, that was an interesting night out," Lucas said, putting his arms around her. "What's the deal with Aisha and Christopher? Do they hate each other or like each other?"

"I think Eesh really does like him, but she can't admit it to herself yet. She's like a train, you know? She's on track, going a certain direction, and you can't try to distract her."

"I'm glad you're not that way," Lucas said, drawing Zoey close.

"Me too," Zoey said.

They kissed for a while, standing under a dripping tree, perfectly private on the quiet, dead-end street.

"I'd better get inside," Zoey said at last. "Parents."

"Yeah, I understand. Not that my parents give a damn if I come home late. They'd probably rather I didn't come home at all." He spoke lightly, trying to keep the bitterness out of his voice.

"I'm sure your dad will lighten up," Zoey said tentatively.

"At least he hasn't said anything in the last few days about shipping me off."

"See? Maybe he's already calming down."

"Probably," Lucas said, smiling to make the lie more believable. His father never forgot anything, and he had never changed his mind that Lucas could remember. But there was always the chance that Lucas's grandfather in Texas would refuse to take him in. His grandfather and his father were family, but not exactly friends.

"I'll think about you all night," Zoey said, gazing at him with her huge, liquid blue eyes.

"And I'll think about you," he said.

"Maybe we could meet in our dreams," she said, half-seriously, half self-mocking.

He smiled. His dreams about Zoey often took on an explicitness that would have shocked her. He wanted her badly, constantly. But there was no way he was going to risk the one decent relationship in his life by asking for something she didn't want to give. Even though each time she kissed him with her impossibly soft lips, her body pressed to his, he thought he might explode.

"Good night," she said, turning to go down the sidewalk to her front door.

He watched her go, savoring the sight of her, storing up memories of her every movement. "See you tomorrow."

He went around the back of her house and found the dark dirt path that led from her backyard up the steep embankment, under his deck, and around to his front door. He went out onto the deck and looked down, just in time to see in the bright incandescent rectangle of her kitchen window as she walked in, executed a little twirl, and hugged her arms to her.

Her father came in, wearing his bathrobe. He looked at the ceiling and shook his head, obviously teasing her, but she just pranced over, planted a kiss on his cheek, and left the room. Her father stood at the sink, setting up a coffee machine for the morning, a wistful, reminiscing smile on his face.

Lucas turned away. His own house was dark, as it had been for hours. His father was a lobsterman and got up each day before the sun, piloting his boat along the sheer mainland shore, winching up lobster pots, throwing back the undersized lobsters, replacing the bait, and lowering the pots again.

Lucas crept into his house, carefully climbing the stairs as silently as a burglar. It was a small house, just two bedrooms upstairs, a living room and the kitchen downstairs. But he had the use of his own bathroom, and his own private room where he could open and shut the door whenever he chose. It wasn't much, certainly not a third the size of Jake's house or Claire's. Even compared to Zoey's modest house, it was modest. But it beat a dormitory cell at the Youth Authority.

He waited until he had closed the door of his room behind him to turn on the light. A single bed, a white-painted dresser, a scratched wood desk with a rickety chair. The only personal touches were left over from two years ago.

It was a simple, uncluttered room, so the sheet of paper lying on his desk looked almost ostentatious. He stood over it, reading.

YOU ARE ON THE 11:00 FLIGHT
TO HOUSTON. SATURDAY.

He stared at the words, forcing his mind to accept what was there in front of him. Saturday. Flight. Houston.

You are on.

He sat on his bed, holding the paper in his hands.

It had happened. His father was actually kicking him out of the house, just as he'd said he would.

Lucas had hoped his mother might find a way of changing his father's mind, but now he knew he'd been deceiving himself. It was his father who was the absolute ruler in this house, just as he was the absolute master of his boat.

Lucas inhaled. It felt like he had forgotten to breathe these last few minutes. Saturday. Three more days, and on the fourth . . .

No more Chatham Island. No more Maine. No more Zoey.

He would almost be glad, he realized, if it weren't for Zoey. His grandfather was unlike his father. He had gone down a different path. He was a tough old guy, but decent. Not the rigid, moralizing, humorless man Lucas's own father was.

He'd be relieved to go to Texas. Except there was no Zoey in Texas.

For the hundredth time he thought of telling his father the truth, explaining what had really happened two years ago when he had so thoughtlessly confessed to something he didn't do.

But his father would dismiss it as another in a long string of lies. Even his mother wouldn't believe it.

Lucas turned off the light and lay back on his bed, still in his damp clothing, and hugged the meager pillow to his chest. He stared into the darkness and saw that rectangle of light, a picture frame holding the image of Zoey, twirling across her kitchen floor and thinking of him.

LUCAS

Why did I sign that confession? Do you have any idea how many times I've asked myself that question? That question has been with me ever since then, every night as I lay in my rack and listened to my cellmates snore and cry in their sleep. And worse things.

Why did I do it?

Because at the time I was in love with Claire. I would have done anything for her. I mean, my life was no Disney World attraction. My mom and dad live in a state of suspended animation, two bodies sharing the same space but nothing else. Do they

hate each other? I don't
know. Do they still love each
other? I don't know that,
either. I know I never
felt like anything other than
an intruder in my own home. I
was this . . . this creature
that stayed up too late,
and ate too much, and never
did anything right.

Claire was the first person
who ever said she loved me.
She was a beautiful, bril-
liant, perfect being, an angel
who for some reason actually
claimed to care about me.
She could do no wrong. So I
didn't argue as hard as I
should have for her to pull
over and stop the car that
night. I mean, jeez, we could
easily have walked home, but
I didn't want to make her
mad by insisting. I just made

A few jokes About it, hoping she'd get the hint And pull over, but drunks Aren't good At taking hints.

We hit. I climbed out through the bAck window And then I got ClAire out of the cAr. Her foreheAd wAs bloody. I got wAde out, too. Funny, but At the time I thought ClAire wAs the one who wAs bAdly hurt.

But he died very soon After. And she wAs in the hospitAl. I wAs terrified thAt she would die. Confessing wAs like . . . like some offering I wAs mAking to God. pleAse just let her live. I'll do Anything, just let ClAire live.

She lived. Her fAther cAme to see me And sAid he thought I wAs being A mAn

Accepting my responsibility the way I was. He had never thought I had the backbone, but now, he could see that he had misjudged me.

He said he knew my dad was having some financial troubles, and he was a banker, so maybe he could help.

You know what's funny? I didn't even understand what Claire's dad was doing till days later. Honest. I didn't understand he was telling me he'd help my dad, but only as long as I stuck to my confession.

Why did I confess? Because I loved Claire. And because even though I hate him, I love my father, too.

Neither of them ever came to visit me. Or sent letters. Or called.

I fell out of love with Claire over time. But what can you do About your dad? He's still Always your dad.

Ten

After school Zoey went straight from the ferry to Lucas's house. He had skipped school that day, leaving Zoey apprehensive. As the day wore on and her imagination grew wilder and wilder, she became totally preoccupied, even fearful.

She ran straight to his house but hesitated at the front door. She hadn't run into either Mr. or Mrs. Cabral since Lucas had come back from jail. She knew that relations between Lucas and his parents were hostile, and she didn't know whether that hostility transferred to her.

She knocked and waited, trying to look pleasant. The door opened quickly. Mrs. Cabral stood there in the dark interior, wiping her hands on her long apron. She had Lucas's blond hair, made lusterless by streaks of gray. Her face was somber, her eyes expressionless.

"Hi, Mrs. Cabral," Zoey said cheerfully.

"Hello, Zoey," Mrs. Cabral said, showing neither surprise nor any great interest. "How are your parents?"

"They're fine, ma'am. They work too much,

but I guess you and Mr. Cabral know about work, don't you? I mean, I know Mr. Cabral's work is really hard. And yours . . . you know, whatever it is, must be . . ." She took a deep breath. "Is Lucas home?"

"He is in his room."

Not exactly an invitation, Zoey realized. "Um, so, can I go up and see him? Or else could he come down?"

Mrs. Cabral stared thoughtfully at her for a moment. Then, with a shrug, she stood back from the door. "Upstairs."

"Thanks," Zoey said, flashing her best smile. She ran up the stairs. The door to what was clearly the parents' room was open. The other bedroom door was closed. She knocked tentatively.

"Yeah?" a muffled voice answered.

"It's me, Zoey. Let me in."

He opened the door, wearing jeans and no shirt. His face was grim. His eyes were red.

"Are you okay? Are you sick?" Zoey asked.

He closed the door behind her and turned away. "I'm not sick."

She stepped up behind him, wanting to put her arms around him, but the situation made her edgy. She was in his room, and she had never seen his bare chest before, and his mother could be right outside the door. She dropped her hand to her side. "So why weren't you in school?" she asked, feeling frustrated and nervous.

He released a deep sigh and bent over to reach into his wastebasket. He retrieved a crumpled ball of paper and handed it to her. Slowly she unwrinkled it, flattening it on the top of his desk to read the message:

> YOU ARE ON THE 11:00 FLIGHT TO HOUSTON. SATURDAY.

Zoey felt like she had been punched. Her knees gave way and she sat hard on the edge of his bed, still holding the paper. "Your father can't really mean this."

"He means it," Lucas said. He went back to his desk and opened the drawer. He held up an envelope with the logo of United Airlines at the corner. "One-way ticket, of course," he said, with a hint of his old humor. "Not even first class. You'd think when you get banished, the least you'd get is a first-class ticket out of town. I'll probably get stuck sitting between a fat guy and a lady with a screaming baby. Then again, knowing my dad, I should probably be glad it's not Greyhound."

"What can we do?" Zoey asked bleakly.

"Well, I'll tell you, Zoey, I've spent the whole night and the whole day so far asking myself that very question." He slid the ticket back in his desk and shut the drawer with finality. "And the answer is, nothing."

"The answer can't be nothing," Zoey said.

"I could try and get a job, rent an apartment, and support myself. I figured it out. If I stay in school, I could probably work about twenty-five hours a week, if anyone would hire a high school kid with a criminal record, no references, and no experience. After taxes and so on I'd probably take home as much as a hundred, hundred and ten a week. Four hundred fifty dollars a month if I'm lucky. With that I might be able to rent an apartment. Unfortunately, I wouldn't be able to heat it, and here in Maine it's a real good idea to have heat in the winter. Also, there wouldn't be any luxuries like clothing, food . . ."

He flopped backward onto the bed beside her. "Or I could drop out of school and get a job making burgers or working at a minimart. If I worked hard, I could still get somewhere. Make manager and so on in a few years."

"You can't drop out of school," Zoey said firmly.

"I don't want to," he said. "But I don't want to lose you, either. You are the only thing I care about."

Zoey lay against him, resting her cheek on

144

his smooth chest. She could hear his heart beating, rising in tempo as she took his hand and squeezed it tightly.

"I love you, Lucas," she whispered.

"I love you, Zoey," he said, his voice rumbling through his chest.

She kissed the spot where his heart beat, then his collarbone, his neck, his lips as he bent to meet her. It was a kiss full of sweetness, full of her own need and desire. But she sensed a reserve in him, as if he could no longer commit himself completely.

She lay back down on his chest, listening to his heartbeat grow more regular. In his mind, she knew, he was already distancing himself from her. He was trying to save himself from the pain of leaving her by leaving her a little at a time.

Tears filled her eyes and flowed down onto his warm skin, trickling along the curve, rolling over his side to stain his sheet. And after a while she felt him sigh, a despairing sound. His arms tightened around her, drawing her up to him again.

There would be no easy way out. No leaving her a little at a time. They were in it together, to the end, whatever might happen.

Their lips met again, and this time Lucas didn't pull away.

Down on the other side of the field, cheerleaders were shouting something in unison, then throwing their right legs up, their left legs up, and falling on the ground in splits.

Claire watched with detached amusement from her perch on the bleachers. Why did girls want to do that? She certainly never had. Bouncing and shouting in front of a crowd of football fans, obsessing over whether one girl's toe was sufficiently pointed or another girl's smile was truly enthusiastic.

But then, she also didn't understand why guys liked to play football.

She turned her attention back to the line of guys bending over, resting on one knuckle dug into the grass, rear ends raised high in the air. Well, at least that part of the game was all right. Unfortunately, Jake wasn't one of the guys bent over. He was standing in back of the line, arms out from his sides.

There was a chant that amounted to a series of numbers, then everyone started running. Someone gave Jake the ball and he tucked it into his arm and ran. Another guy plowed into him, but Jake spun and ran on. Then two guys jumped him from behind, bringing him crashing down to earth.

Jake got up laughing, shaking his head ruefully. He trotted over toward Claire, pulling off his helmet as he ran, and removing a slobbery piece of plastic from his mouth.

"See that?" he yelled as he came closer.

"Yes. I hope it didn't hurt."

"Hurt?" he said as if it was a ridiculous suggestion. "I broke the first tackle and carried the second tackle with me for another five yards. I gained fifteen yards; that's a first down and then some. I'm ready for the game Friday. Big-time ready."

He ran up the bleachers and sat down beside her, sweaty but exuberant.

"So you're saying what you did was good?" Claire said.

He squinted at her doubtfully. "You're not a football fan, are you?"

"Mmmm, I guess you wouldn't say *fan*."

Jake laughed good-naturedly. "In other words, you know absolutely nothing about the game."

"I know it involves a ball. And I thought several of your teammates had nice butts."

Jake winced and shook his head. "No. No one on the team has a nice butt. The game is not about guys' butts. It's war, it's destruction, it's about power and taking the other guy's territory away from him, advancing, penetrating. Like Napoleon at Waterloo."

"Napoleon lost the battle of Waterloo," Claire pointed out.

"Yeah, well, we're playing South Portland on Friday, so it's probably a pretty good example to use," he said wryly. "They've beaten us every year since . . . actually, since Waterloo, come to think of it."

"Isn't it depressing to think you're going to lose a game?"

"Haven't you heard? It's not whether you win or lose, it's how you play the game." Jake gave her one of his most wonderful smiles. "Sure it's depressing, but their school is twice the size of ours, so we don't feel too depressed. Besides, we might win. Their quarterback could get hit by a bus."

"I've never been to a game," Claire admitted. "I guess if I'm going to be your girlfriend, I'll have to go to all of them."

Jake looked down and kicked mud from his cleats. "Zoey only came to three or four during the year, usually," he said. "But I think I finally got her to more or less understand the game."

Claire was silent, and the silence stretched for several minutes while the rest of the team ran plays. "I guess it's way too soon for you to be over her," she said softly.

"Yes and no," Jake said. "Most of me is just so glad you and I are together that I almost don't care. But it still hurts, you know. I mean, no one likes to get dumped." His face grew dark. "Especially not when you're getting dumped for someone like Lucas."

Claire put her hand on Jake's arm. "I'm glad you've managed to stay out of fights with him. I was worried you might do something stupid."

"I would have, except I don't really need to,"

Jake said. "That's one of the lessons you learn in football. Don't take unnecessary hits, and don't apply unnecessary hits. When the man is down, don't pile on. If he's down, that's all that counts. And Lucas," he said the name with a sneer, "is out of the game."

"What do you mean?" Claire asked, feeling uneasy.

"My dad talks to Mr. Cabral just about every day. Mr. Cabral fuels up at our marina. My dad says Lucas has a one-way plane ticket out of town as of Saturday. Good-bye, Lucas." Jake smiled a cold, unpleasant smile. "Zoey may have dumped me, but the guy she dumped me for has less than three more days before he's history."

A fierce current of joy and relief flooded Claire's mind, almost taking her breath away with its intensity. Lucas, gone in three days! It was like a miracle. With him gone, there would be no one around to reveal the truth. No one but Benjamin, and he had no proof, just guesses. Her secret was safe. Safe from everyone, and most of all, safe from Jake.

She leaned over and started to kiss Jake, but he pulled back.

"I'm all sweaty and dirty," he protested, "and my breath probably smells like Joe Bolt's shoe since he stuck it into my mouth on that last play."

"Joe Bolt," she said thoughtfully. "Is he the

one with the nice behind?"

"Claire," Jake said reproachfully, "we are all very, very tough guys and manly men and all. No one on the team has anything nice. Except maybe me."

He kissed her, holding his body away.

"McRoyan!" the coach yelled up at him from the field. "Are you practicing or are you making out?"

"Right there, Coach!" Jake yelled back.

"Tell him you don't need practice, you're making out just fine."

He smiled, and then she noticed he was blushing and looking awkwardly down at his cleats again. "You know, Claire, I don't know if I should say this or anything, but, you know, I'm really . . . I mean, I really am starting to like you. A lot. I mean, I always liked you, just now it's more. And different. You know."

Claire felt strangely touched. There was something so sincere and utterly without deception about Jake. In a million years he would never lie to her.

Not like she was lying to him.

The thought stabbed her and made her clench her fist.

"I guess I shouldn't have said that," Jake said, looking embarrassed. "I mean, even though we've known each other forever, we've only been *together* for a little while."

"No, I'm glad you said it, Jake. Very glad."

"McRoyan, for cripes' sake, what the hell are you doing?" The coach's voice was rising in exasperation.

Jake rolled his eyes. "I have to get back to the other manly men."

"Here," Claire said, grabbing the front of his jersey and pulling him down to her. She gave him a long, deep kiss. "Give the manly men something to be jealous of."

He bounded down the bleachers, greeted by rude catcalls from his teammates. She watched him as he rejoined his team.

It would be easy to find the words to tell him the truth. *Jake, I was driving the car when Wade was killed.* But it was impossible to imagine what she would say after those ten words.

Eleven

"Morning, morning, morning," Nina said the next morning in a low, grumpy voice. She flopped onto the bench beside Zoey, pulled a Lucky Strike from a pack in her purse, and stuck it in her mouth, drawing deeply on the unlit cigarette. She propped her Doc Martens on the back of the next seat and cast a glance around the ferry. "What's it been, two weeks? Not even, and already I can announce that I officially hate school. I mean, seriously, what are we all doing out of bed at this hour? And I was up late last night trying to figure out how it is that the Russians could be good guys in World War I, then bad guys at the beginning of World War II, changing again to good guys halfway through, then as soon as the war was over they were bad again, up until a few years ago when they switched back to good. I think there should be a law: You pick a side, good or bad, then you have to stick with it. Hey, Eesh. You're a senior. What's the deal with the Russians? Good, bad, or just indecisive?"

Aisha stopped in front of Zoey and shook

her head. "You look bad, Zoey. What's the matter, are you sick?"

"You're sick?" Nina asked in surprise, looking at Zoey more closely. "Why didn't you say something?"

"I'm not sick," Zoey said in a low whisper.

"You look sick," Aisha said flatly. "If it's catching, stay away from me."

"If it's catching but it's not too painful, come closer. I wouldn't mind a few sick days," Nina said.

"It's not that," Zoey said. "It's Lucas."

"Don't tell me you two are fighting," Aisha said.

"His father is making him leave. He . . ." Zoey's voice broke. "Saturday. He's leaving Saturday."

"*This* Saturday?" Nina asked.

Zoey nodded.

"Can he do that?" Aisha asked. "I mean, Lucas is still his son."

"He's over eighteen," Zoey explained. "His dad could just kick him out the door if he wanted to. Lucas says at least his dad found him a place to stay, with his grandfather until he can finish school there."

"Texas, right?" Aisha said.

"Some crappy little town," Zoey muttered. "More than two thousand miles away. Two thousand miles."

Nina scratched her head uncomfortably and

chewed the end of her unlit cigarette. She had never seen Zoey so upset before, about anything. Zoey was always sunshine to Nina's rain. It was unnatural having her on the edge of tears, but obviously so cried out that no tears would come. She glanced over at Aisha, who just shrugged and bit her lip. *Aisha's probably dying to say I told you so,* Nina thought.

"Isn't there any way to get Mr. Cabral not to do this?" Aisha asked. "I mean, I guess Lucas has tried and all."

Zoey nodded mutely. The ferry whistle blew, and the boat began to draw away from the dock. Nina saw Jake glance in their direction, his eyes softening for Zoey, then growing hard and pitiless. Claire was close by him. She stared for a moment, too.

"I can't take it," Zoey said in her low, trembling whisper. "It's not right. No one should tear people apart who love each other."

Nina put her arm around her friend's shoulders. Aisha sat close on Zoey's other side and took Zoey's hand. Zoey found a few extra tears, which fell softly on her books, forming little dark spots on La Langue Française.

"What am I going to do?" Zoey wondered. "I can't go with him, can I? Where would I stay? How could I still finish school?"

Nina made eye contact with Aisha over Zoey's bowed head.

"He told me yesterday. I went up to his house because he wasn't in school. I guess he figures why bother for just two or three days. I spoke to his mother, but Lucas says she's totally under his dad's thumb. He showed me the note his father left him, not even anything on it but the time the flight leaves. His family is so cold, you wouldn't believe it."

Nina was about to break the tension with a joke about Claire, something along the lines of knowing all about cold families, but again she saw Claire across the open deck, stealing a furtive glance at Zoey. Claire's lips were pressed into a thin line, and she looked away quickly when she saw Nina watching her.

Very strange, Nina thought. *She acts like she knows why Zoey is sad*. Then again, it was a small island. Claire probably did know.

Claire glanced back again. Weird, especially given that there was an amazing pile of those really tall clouds on the horizon. Why wasn't Claire staring up at them?

"Just tonight, then tomorrow will be the last night I have with him," Zoey said, sounding hopeless. "I really love him, you guys. I really do. We kissed for hours after he told me. Hours, but it still seemed like no time at all, and I could tell he was trying to pull away from me emotionally. I can't blame him. I wish I could pull away from him, but I can't."

"This is true love," Aisha said darkly. "It's great for a while, but it always seems to lead to pain in the end." She put her hand on Zoey's. "I guess you couldn't stop yourself. Maybe there really is such a thing as fate. Maybe you were just doomed to go through this."

"It isn't doom, Eesh," Zoey said through her tears. "I mean, I'd still do it all over again, even knowing . . . knowing . . ." She succumbed to sobs.

Aisha looked troubled. She gave Zoey a disbelieving look, but Nina could see doubt there, too.

For her part, Nina felt the beginnings of tears. It had suddenly occurred to her that this could happen to any guy and girl. What if Benjamin were suddenly to disappear from her life? Not that he was exactly *in* her life. But what if she knew she might never see him again?

The first tear welled in her eye and trundled down her cheek.

"Both of you stop it, now," Aisha said, but not harshly. "How are we supposed to get through the whole day at school when we start off weeping on the ferry?"

"Sorry," Zoey murmured. She sat up straight and wiped her eyes.

Nina rubbed her friend's back slowly. "It will all work out somehow. Won't it, Aisha?"

"Sure, of course it will."

"Some dumb parent can't stop true love, can he?" Nina challenged. "Look at Romeo and Juliet.

Their parents tried to stop them, didn't they?"

"They ended up dead," Aisha said.

"Oh, right. Well, I know this for a fact—Wilma's parents never did approve of Fred."

Aisha rolled her eyes to the sky. "Nina, if I ever need to be comforted, remind me not to come to you."

"Don't tell me," Benjamin said, holding up his hand. "It's . . . um, sloppy joes made with ground turkey . . . green beans . . . and, um, I want to be sure . . ." He sniffed the air carefully. "Cherry . . . no, raspberry Jell-O."

The old woman behind the lunch counter shook her head in amazement and piled Benjamin's tray high. Benjamin smiled in her general direction and pushed his tray along on the stainless steel railing.

"Okay, not to be dumb," Aisha said, just behind him in the cafeteria line, "but how *do* you do that? I mean, are you telling me you can *smell* raspberry Jell-O from ten feet away with the air full of sloppy joe and perfume and body odor?"

"It's easy," Benjamin said out of the side of his mouth. "They list the school lunches in the paper at the beginning of each week. Today sloppy joes, green beans, and Jell-O."

"The paper specified *raspberry* Jell-O?"

"No." Benjamin dug his lunch ticket out of his pocket and handed it to the cashier. "The guys in front of us asked what flavor it was. It's always useful to have an air of mystery about you when you're a discriminated-against minority. Don't you think?"

Aisha took his arm and led him across the crowded lunchroom to an empty table. It was one of the things Benjamin couldn't do alone, not unless he just wanted to grab the first vacant seat he stumbled into. Classrooms were different; steps could usually be counted. His English class was one step in, left seventeen steps, right nine steps, and his desk would be in the back row, halfway across the room. To get to the room itself would be sixty-three steps along the hall, up four flights of stairs, right forty-eight steps.

But in the lunchroom, tables tended to get shoved around more, chairs reassembled in different groupings each day, so whoever happened to be nearest the cashier, usually an islander but often other kids, would grab Benjamin's elbow and ask where he wanted to go or whom he wanted to sit with.

"Table's to your left," Aisha said.

He heard her sit down at the seat roughly across the table from him. He aimed his sunglasses in her direction. "Aren't you sitting with Zoey today?"

"What, you don't like my company?"

Hearing her voice again, he readjusted the aim of his shades. "I've always enjoyed your company," he said. "I was just making sure this wasn't a pity date because I don't have Claire to sit with anymore."

"You're a very prickly guy, you know that?" Aisha said.

Benjamin smiled. "I think that's why I don't have Claire to sit with anymore."

Aisha sighed. "Actually, I don't want to sit with your sister because she's just too depressing. Don't tell her I said that, but all she's done all day long is sniffle."

Benjamin frowned. "What's the matter?"

"Oh, great. You don't know? So I'm the one telling you?"

"Telling me what?"

Aisha sighed again and rearranged her silverware. "You probably *should* know," she said reluctantly. "You are Zoey's brother, and besides, I don't think she's trying to keep it a big secret or anything. I think she's just too close to having a nervous breakdown. It's Lucas."

"Oh, a romantic problem," Benjamin said. "What's up? They can't agree on whether they should get engaged?"

"Mr. Cabral is kicking Lucas out. He has to go live with his grandfather in Texas somewhere."

"What?"

"Yeah, you know. Lucas is a juvenile delinquent who has embarrassed his family or whatever. You know Mr. Cabral. He's like, uptight father squared."

Benjamin threw his fork down on his tray, making a clattering noise. He cursed under his breath, finishing with *that selfish bitch*.

"Who's a selfish bitch?" Aisha demanded. "Zoey?"

"No, no," Benjamin said quickly. "Of course not. Zoey's anything but selfish. Poor kid. Man, she got herself in the middle of it this time."

"I told her running around with Lucas Cabral would lead to trouble," Aisha said.

"Zoey's too much of a romantic to listen to sensible warnings," Benjamin said affectionately.

"Exactly. If she'd listened to reason and common sense, none of this would have happened."

Benjamin barked a short, dismissive laugh. "Aisha, if people listened to reason and common sense, we'd all still be walking around dragging our knuckles, eating bugs, and talking in grunts. We'd be baboons. Football players."

"I don't see Zoey crying and sobbing for twenty-four hours straight as part of the march of civilization," Aisha said sarcastically.

"Yeah, well, neither is sitting on the sidelines saying *I told you so*. I'm sure when the first caveman burned himself trying to start a fire with a couple of sticks, some smartass was there saying, *Hey, I told you not to play with fire*."

He winced as Aisha slapped the table. "You know how I said you were prickly? Leave off the *l* and the *y*."

Benjamin held up his hands placatingly. "Aisha, I wasn't talking about you. We were just having a discussion."

"I know you're not talking about me," Aisha snapped. "We're talking about your sister, who is four tables away looking like someone drained all the blood out of her. Damn. Nina's giving me a come-help-me-out look. I have to go."

"Tell Zoey to be cool; Mr. Cabral will probably lighten up eventually."

He heard the scrape of Aisha's chair. "I don't know how much he's going to lighten up between now and Saturday," she said doubtfully.

"Saturday?" Benjamin said, feeling a jolt of concern. "You don't mean as in the day after tomorrow?"

"As in the morning after tomorrow," Aisha said.

BENJAMIN

Zoey is my little sister. That's just a biological fact. I was born a year and seven months before her. And all the time we were growing up, I was the traditional big brother, which, as I understood it, meant that I had two major duties: First, I was ~~reuqired~~ required by law to tease her. About her hair, her body, her ideas, her clothes, her friends, and anything else that came to mind.

The other thing a big brother did was protect. I was supposed to protect her from anyone or anything that might threaten her. That was ~~su-posed~~ supposed to be a lifelong job.

My career as a big brother didn't last long, though. I was twelve when I lost my sight. I'm not supposed to say that, by the way. "Lost my sight" is negative, you see. The therapist who taught me my basic coping skills wanted me to say that I had "become differently abled." I was only twelve, but I still knew b.s. when I heard it.

Anyway. I was twelve, Zoey was ten, and all of a sudden I wasn't a "big" brother anymore. I fell behind at school till I had to race just to stay even with her. I couldn't protect anyone. Not even myself. If you've never been anyone's big brother, you don't know how pathetic it makes you feel to ~~duddenly~~ suddenly need your baby sister to lead you to the men's-room door at the mall, or find your belt because you don't remember precisely where you hung it. Or pipe up in her brave little voice and tell some punk to leave you alone, stop picking on my brother, he needs his cane.

And yet, I discovered that from time to time there were ways I could help her. I pushed myself so hard at school that soon she didn't have to pity me, or worry about how I'd feel if ~~agw~~ she was better than me at something. I drilled myself endlessly to handle getting around town and the ferry and the school, so she wouldn't have to spend her life being my guide. I worked to free her from me and, as you might expect, I freed myself at the same time.

I still can't beat guys up for her, but from time to time, in little ways, I do still get to be her big brother.

Twelve

Usually Nina, Aisha, and Zoey met at the end of the school day to walk together down to the ferry landing. They met on the front steps of the three-story brick behemoth, and since there was always an hour to kill till the four o'clock ferry, they would wander the tiny shops of downtown Weymouth, or stop in at a hangout for ice cream.

But the usual had been suspended for now.

Nina and Aisha watched as Zoey came down the front steps, arm in arm with Lucas. *Like Siamese twins*, Nina thought. *Like they've been Superglued together*.

Not that she could blame either of them. They had tonight and tomorrow, and that was it.

"Hi, guys," Zoey said in her worn, soft voice.

"Hi, you two," Nina said.

"Are you coming?" Zoey asked.

Nina flashed a quick glance at Aisha. "No, I don't think so. Why don't you two go on ahead, and Eesh and I will see you on the ferry."

Zoey didn't argue, just smiled a pathetically

grateful smile and walked on, still hanging on to Lucas.

"You know, Aisha," Nina said, "I'm starting to think you're right. Why would anyone deliberately put themselves in a position to suffer like that?"

"Oh, so now *you* think I'm right?" Aisha said grumpily.

"I'm just saying, what's so great about falling in love if you end up like Zoey and Lucas?"

Nina hopped down off the steps and popped an unlit cigarette in her mouth. They began walking across the field, the shortcut to town. The football team was running around at one end of the field. Closer at hand, a less-organized-looking group of girls were learning how to advance soccer balls. Nina recognized Christopher, wearing bike shorts and a rugby shirt, teaching the finer points.

"I'm glad someone agrees with me," Aisha said. "Benjamin called me a baboon."

"A baboon? Why?"

"And on the ferry this morning did you hear Zoey? *I'd still do it all over again, even knowing boohoo*? Even now she acts like she did the right thing."

Nina took a drag on the Lucky Strike. "Love is a many-splendored thing, Eesh," she said philosophically. "Better to have loved and lost than never to have loved at all."

"Oh, shut up. I don't see you trying it."

An image of Benjamin leaning close, his lips nearly touching her ear, came to Nina's mind. It was replaced by another image, of Benjamin saying, "I never thought of you as a romantic type, Nina. Is it anyone in particular, or is that none of my business?"

"I'm like you, Eesh," Nina said wistfully. "Too big a coward to take the chance of getting dumped on."

"So now I'm a coward," Aisha said.

"Better than a baboon," Nina pointed out.

Aisha stopped and planted her hands on her hips. "Obviously everyone is just going to keep picking on me."

Nina looked at her friend in puzzlement. Suddenly Aisha was upset, and Nina had no real idea why.

"I'm not a coward," Aisha ranted. "I've gone out with lots of guys, unlike you, may I point out, Ms. Too-cool-for-everyone. I'm *not* afraid, I'm just sensible. See, I don't let other people decide what I'm going to do, or whom I'm going to go out with. That does not make me a baboon or a caveman."

"No, I—" Nina began.

"But everyone is just going to keep picking on me until I go out with him. You, Zoey, Benjamin, my mother."

"Go out with who?" Nina asked.

"Like you don't know. Don't waste your time

166

trying child psychology on me; I'm not a child."

Or a baboon, Nina added silently.

"But just to shut everyone up, just so everyone will finally leave me alone in peace, I'll do it. All right? I'll do it."

Nina was about to ask what Aisha was going to do, but her friend spun on her heel and began marching across the field. Aisha stopped in the middle of the soccer players and planted herself in front of Christopher.

"Oh," Nina said. She flopped down on the grass, watching. Of course. Duh.

Aisha evidently asked a question, and Christopher evidently answered, because after a few seconds Aisha came marching back. Nina got up, picking bits of grass off the backs of her thighs.

"We're going out tomorrow night," Aisha said. "Are you happy now?"

"You just went right up and asked him out?" Nina said wonderingly. "Just like that?"

"Yeah," Aisha answered, trying unsuccessfully to stop a smile. "Just like that."

"And it worked, huh?" Nina asked thoughtfully.

"Of course," Aisha said. "I don't believe in all that coy girly stuff. That's why *I* won't end up like Zoey. Just because you go out with a guy, that doesn't mean anything. I just did it so you all would leave me alone. It does not mean I'm interested in him."

"Just go up and say, *do you want to go out with me*?" Nina muttered.

"Come on. I need something to wear, and the ferry's in forty-five minutes."

"It's really only been a few days," Claire said. "But I feel like . . . I feel a lot for him."

"As you pointed out, you've known Jake your whole life," Dr. Kendall said in her neutral, nonjudgmental psychiatrist's voice.

Claire shifted in her seat, making the leather creak. Dr. Kendall believed there was significance in everything, even shifting from one position to another because your left butt cheek was numb. "I know, but we were never close. Once when Zoey—that's his former girlfriend—was out of town, I kind of took a run at him. You know, a friendly kiss."

Dr. Kendall nodded.

"Maybe a *very* friendly kiss. But I was going with Benjamin, and Jake was with Zoey. But now that we've all broken up, things are different."

"Are you saying that you never really cared for Benjamin?"

Claire reflected for a moment, as memories came drifting up to her consciousness. "No, I really did care for Benjamin."

"Yet it was you who broke off the relationship with him."

Claire grinned mischievously. "Everyone needs

168

a little variety. Benjamin was old news. Besides, he has annoying habits that get on my nerves. He is the pickiest person sometimes. Not to mention suspicious. And now with Jake I'm so much happier. I know it's sudden and all, but already I think I feel more for him than I ever did for Benjamin."

"I'm happy for you," Dr. Kendall said.

"Yeah. I'm happy, too," Claire said, feeling vaguely dissatisfied even as she said it.

"He is the brother of the boy who died in the accident, isn't he?"

"Uh-huh. Wade was Jake's brother."

Dr. Kendall fell into one of her long, dragging silences.

"I suppose you think there's something psychological going on there," Claire said mockingly.

Dr. Kendall smiled and lifted her shoulders.

"You mean like I'm going out with Jake to make up for his losing Wade? That's stretching it pretty far, isn't it?"

"That would be pretty far-fetched. Unless you had some reason to feel guilty over Wade's death."

Claire's breath caught in her throat. She forced a cough to cover her gasp. What the hell had made Dr. Kendall say that? When she was done coughing, she apologized. "Sorry. I think I breathed in some dust."

"I'll have to ask the cleaning crew to dust more thoroughly. I was just wondering whether you felt any guilt over the death of Jake's brother. People sometimes experience guilt even over things for which they bear no responsibility," Dr. Kendall said.

"I guess that's true," Claire said. "But no, I don't feel any guilt. Except maybe, you know, feeling a little strange that I survived and someone else died."

"That's also a very common feeling."

Claire smiled broadly. "So, I'm still not crazy? Damn, and I've tried so hard."

Dr. Kendall put on the strained smile she wore whenever Claire used the word crazy. "I already gave you my opinion, Claire. You're a strikingly well-balanced person for a teenager in this day and age. You don't use drugs, you aren't promiscuous, you get along well with your father, and I believe you have adjusted well to the death of your mother. The fact that you can't remember the accident only means that you suffered a concussion that affected short-term memory."

"You probably kept me sane," Claire said insincerely.

"Our hour is nearly up. Have there been any more dreams about the accident?"

"Nope. Sorry. Although I had a dream about Kramer, you know, the guy on *Seinfeld*? That was pretty gross. I could tell you about it and throw in a few details to make it more interesting."

"Another time," Dr. Kendall said. "And no memory flashes? Nothing new on that front?"

"No. It's still as much of a blank as ever."

Thirteen

Claire was not on the four-o'clock ferry, much to Benjamin's annoyance. Then he realized where she was: the psychiatrist Claire thought no one knew about. The one she'd been seeing since her mother died. Damn, he cursed himself, he should have tried to catch her there as she came out. That would have given him quite a nice little edge.

But then, he didn't know where the shrink's office was, so he would have had to be led. And then, a blind guy couldn't "accidentally" run into anyone who didn't want to be run into. He would have needed someone else along to act as his eyes, and that was unacceptable.

Instead he went to Claire and Nina's house just before seven o'clock, minutes before he knew that Claire would arrive on the later ferry. It would be tricky because he would have to avoid Nina and Mr. Geiger and somehow get to Claire alone.

He counted the steps from the corner of Center, right, with the sound of surf to his left. He found the familiar gate and opened it.

Did Mr. Geiger know he and Claire had broken up? Probably not. But Nina certainly knew, and she was bound to think that he was there to beg Claire to come back to him.

He knocked on the front door.

"Hey, Benjamin, haven't seen you around here in some days."

Mr. Geiger. Benjamin was relieved. "Hi, Mr. Geiger. Is Claire around?"

"No, she's not home yet. But I expect she'll be up from the dock in a few minutes." He ushered Benjamin inside. The two of them had always gotten along well. "Can you stay for dinner? Love to have you."

"No, thanks, I've already eaten. You know we middle-class types eat dinner earlier than you folks with the lifestyle of the rich and famous."

Mr. Geiger let the remark go with good humor. "This rich and famous person has some work to do. Foreclosing on widows and orphans, as you always say. But Nina's upstairs. You want me to call her down?"

"No, no," Benjamin said quickly. "I'll just head on up and wait for Claire in her room, if that's all right with you."

"You know the way," Mr. Geiger said.

He did. Nineteen steps up. Turn right and follow the railing around. This was the tricky part, passing the door to Nina's room. If it was open, she'd come out and press him for some explanation. He heard music, muffled, and Nina's voice, singing along slightly off-key. Good, the door was closed. Now, fifteen more steps to Claire's room.

He found the bed and sat down, trying to look casual. A moment later he heard the front door of the house opening, closing. A pause, then a light tread climbing the steps. Good, just one person. She hadn't brought Jake home with her.

That would certainly have made things interesting.

"Benjamin. What are you doing here?"

"Hi, Claire."

"Hello, Benjamin. What are you doing here?"

Benjamin stood up and squared his shoulders. "We have to talk."

He heard Claire make a derisive noise. "I never thought you'd come begging, Benjamin. I'm with Jake now."

"That's not why I came," Benjamin said calmly, although her tone had hurt him. "Do you know that Lucas is leaving the island on Saturday?"

"I may have heard something about it," Claire said.

"You feel relieved that he's going?"

"I don't think I feel relieved, Benjamin. I'm not sorry he's going, though. No one on the island wants him around. The sooner he's gone, the sooner everything will get back to normal."

"Normal," Benjamin repeated wryly.

"Is that what you came here for? To ask me

how I feel about Lucas leaving?"

Benjamin considered his answer for a moment. "In a way, yes. I was curious about how you felt, knowing that Lucas was going to suffer still more for something you did."

"That again?" Claire snapped angrily.

"That again," he answered quietly. "That again, that forever until you decide to tell the truth, Claire."

"Get out of here."

"He spent two years in reform school—well, let's call it what it was, jail. He spent two years in jail for something he didn't do. Maybe you didn't realize what was happening then. Maybe you really didn't remember back then; I'm willing to believe that. But you remember now."

"I don't remember anything, Benjamin. I know you think you're just the smartest person on the planet, but you can't read minds. You can't see inside me." She laughed cruelly. "In fact, Benjamin, you can't even look into my eyes, can you?"

Benjamin actually stepped back, stunned by her sudden fury. She had never resorted to cheap ridicule like that before. "I see enough," he said. "I know you remember."

"Why the hell do you care? Why is any of this *your* business? Why don't you deal with your own screwed-up life and stay out of mine? What's Lucas to you?"

"He's someone my sister cares about," Benjamin said.

"Oh, just get out of here."

"Lies have already cost Lucas two years of his life—"

"—I said get out!"

"And now they're going to cost him more."

"Benjamin, I swear to God I'm going to push you down the steps!"

"And they're going to cost my little sister a broken heart."

"Where are the violins? A broken heart? I can't believe I'm hearing this from your mouth, Benjamin. What do you know about anything? You wouldn't know a broken heart if you tripped over it."

A wave of sadness swept over him. She wasn't going to back down. He had failed. He felt his resolve collapsing. "I might know a broken heart," Benjamin said softly. He took a deep breath. "I'm surprised by you, Claire. I didn't think you were this far gone. I never would have believed it of you."

"Get over yourself, Benjamin."

"I could go and tell Mr. Cabral the truth," Benjamin said halfheartedly.

"And you think he'd believe you? You think he'd just accept your intuition that Lucas is innocent?" Claire laughed scornfully.

Benjamin shook his head. "No. He wouldn't believe me. He wouldn't believe Lucas, even if Lucas did try to tell him. There's only one person that anyone will believe, Claire, and that's you. You're the only one who would have nothing to gain."

"Nothing to gain," she repeated.

"Except that you would be telling the truth. This has all been about dishonesty. First Lucas lying to cover up for you, now you lying to protect yourself." He loaded his voice with weary scorn. "I never thought I would feel contempt for you, Claire."

She laughed. "You don't feel contempt for me, Benjamin."

He could feel that she was closer, feel the warmth of her body within inches of his own. Her fingers grazed his chin. He jerked his head away. But then her hand lay against his chest. He wanted to pull away, but he didn't.

She brushed his lips with her own and he moved closer, craving the contact, needing to feel her mouth on his again. But she was gone.

"See? You're not nearly as hard to figure out as you imagine, Benjamin. Now get out."

Claire listened to the sound of his slow, measured tread descending the stairs. She started to smile, but her lip was quivering. Her hands were shaking and she clasped them together to control them.

That bastard. That nosy, pushy, arrogant bastard. She *should* have pushed him down the stairs. She should have. He deserved it. Coming around here and accusing her of things. Trying to make her feel guilty.

She tore off the shirt she had worn to school and rummaged in her dresser for a sweatshirt. She realized she was throwing clothing across the room. She grabbed the next shirt that came to hand and slipped it on.

Guilt. What did she have to feel guilty about? She hadn't known. She had not remembered. It wasn't her fault that Lucas decided to be a knight on a white horse and confess. She hadn't asked him to. And if she had known the truth, she would have told everyone. She never, never would have let him go to jail for her. She wasn't that kind of person at all. That would have been cowardly, and she was no coward.

But she hadn't remembered.

Until just last week.

It was too late! It was too late to change everything. Even if she told Mr. Cabral the truth, it wasn't like he and Lucas would suddenly be best friends. Going off to Texas was probably the best thing for Lucas. He'd be better off away from the island. He would.

And as for Zoey's broken heart . . .

Well, Zoey hadn't minded breaking Jake's heart, had she? Why was this any different? In fact, if Claire were to go around blurting out the truth, that would just hurt Jake even more. And he was the main victim, not Lucas. Lucas had always been trouble. Jake was the sweetest guy on earth. He deserved to have some happiness.

Saturday morning it would be over, Claire told herself. Saturday morning it would all be over. Lucas would be gone. No one would ever ask any embarrassing questions of her father. She and Jake would still be together. Zoey would be ready to forget all about Lucas.

That would be best for everyone. History could not be rewritten.

No one would know but her and her father.

And Benjamin, who could do nothing about it.

She heard Nina's voice yelling up to her that dinner was ready.

She wasn't hungry, but it would look strange not to eat. A quick dinner, then over to see Jake. Jake would help her to forget all about Benjamin, and Zoey crying on the ferry, and the image of Lucas climbing on a plane and disappearing, this time for good.

Jake. How good it would feel to be with him and put Benjamin out of her mind.

Fourteen

"I've never shown this to anyone," Zoey said later that same evening, pulling a heavy bound pad from the drawer of her desk. "I've been writing in it for years."

"I didn't know you wrote," Lucas said, sitting on the edge of her bed.

"Well, I write, I just never finish anything," Zoey admitted.

"What do you write?"

Zoey made a face and smiled self-deprecatingly. "You'll just laugh."

"I promise I won't." He crossed his heart and looked solemn.

"I've written the first chapter of a romance novel about twenty-five times. Always chapter one, or else just a single scene. I have about a hundred and twenty pages altogether."

Lucas smiled. "Romance novel? You mean like those books with the covers where some half-naked guy is groping a woman whose dress is falling off?"

"Yeah, and the woman always has these big

double-*D*-cup buffers squeezing out of a *B*-cup bodice. Except in mine the heroine is always normal size. Maybe even a little on the small end of the spectrum."

"And how about the hero?" Lucas asked. "Six five, big squared-off chest about a yard wide, smoldering dark eyes?"

"Lately he's been more like five-ten. But he has a nice chest. And he does have smoldering dark eyes."

Lucas gave her an exaggeratedly smoldering look. "Like this?"

"Smoldering, not nearsighted," Zoey teased. Then she squealed as Lucas grabbed her and threw her back on the bed. She was still giggling and squirming when he kissed her. She closed her eyes and put her arms around his neck.

"By the way, they're not on the small end of the spectrum," Lucas said when they paused for air.

"Trust me," Zoey said. "Padding." She felt his hand move, and she caught her breath.

"Mmm, not padding," Lucas said in a husky voice.

"Lucas . . ."

"Yes?"

"That's, um . . . it's, oh . . . oh, what I mean is . . ."

"Tell me, in this romance novel you're working on, do the hero and the heroine ever make love?"

"Um, well, no. I mean, she never has."

"Never?" he asked, looking at her skeptically.

"I think I would know if the heroine had ever done it," Zoey said.

"Not even with . . . with the previous hero?" Lucas asked.

"No, not ever," Zoey said, feeling a blush rise up her neck. "She's not ready. Besides, that part always comes much later in the book after the hero and the heroine have either been married in the cathedral, or maybe been thrown into a dungeon together where they think they're going to get their heads chopped off the next day."

"Oh. Doesn't your hero *want* to, you know, make love?"

Zoey captured his hand with hers and raised it to her lips, kissing the tips of his fingers. "The hero pretty much always wants to make love. And it's not like the heroine doesn't. She has heaving-bosom syndrome, which is very common in romance novels. But being the heroine, she has to maintain a grip."

"Poor hero," Lucas said.

"Not really," Zoey said. "He just needs to learn that it's not always about having. Romance is about wanting."

Lucas made a pained face. "What if he explodes?"

"He won't," Zoey said confidently.

He kissed her deeply, a heart-stopping kiss

181

that left them both breathless. "What if our heroine explodes?" Lucas asked in a low voice.

"Now that is . . . oh . . . a real possibility," Zoey said, closing her eyes. "But the thing to worry about is that if the hero does that again, he's going to get his hand smacked."

"Did I do it wrong?"

"No, no, you definitely did it right. Believe me. Only don't do it again." She pushed him back gently. "Maybe we should take a time-out. We have plenty of time."

Lucas's face fell, and instantly Zoey realized what she'd said was untrue. They didn't have plenty of time.

Lucas sat back and smiled at her ruefully, shaking his head. "Bad choice of words. It can happen to any writer, I guess."

"What are we going to do, Lucas?" Zoey asked, her voice betraying the desperation that came flooding over her again.

He raised his hands in a gesture of helplessness. "I don't know. I keep thinking there's something I've overlooked, some way to make it all work."

"There has to be a way," Zoey said. "It's ridiculous that some mistake you made two years ago would screw up our lives, maybe forever."

He nodded and averted his eyes.

"I'm sorry, I shouldn't have brought that up," Zoey said. "You know I think that's all ancient history. I know you're sorry for what happened, and you've already paid for it once. I just don't see why you should have to still go on paying. It's not fair."

But Lucas didn't respond. He pulled away and rested his elbows on his knees, hanging his head.

"Did I . . . did I say something wrong, Lucas?" She put her hand on his shoulder, and after a moment's hesitation he covered her hand with his.

"No. No, you didn't say anything wrong." He forced a smile and gently caressed her cheek. "Let's just not talk about it anymore. Heroes and heroines shouldn't be sad."

"Hmm," Jake muttered, thinking over Claire's question. "I guess red. It's bright, it doesn't fool around, it says, Look at me, I am definitely red. How about you?"

"Blue," Claire said without hesitation. "Blue sky, blue water."

"Can a red and a blue get along?" Jake wondered.

"Together we make purple," Claire pointed out. "Now, greens and yellows, no way. You'd get brown."

"Hmm," Jake said.

"Hmm," Claire replied.

This is good, Claire realized. *This is good, and something I could never really do with*

Benjamin. She was walking along the west beach barefoot, holding hands with Jake, the two of them swinging their arms back and forth. Talking about nothing at all. Just enjoying the stars and the moon and being together. With Benjamin she had always been so serious.

No, that wasn't really fair, but it was how she felt. And as mean as it might be to think it, it was nice to be able to share the visual universe with someone, both of you enjoying the size of the moon, or the way the lights of Weymouth sparkled on the bay.

"Between Guns 'n' Roses and U2," Jake said.

"I have to go with U2."

"Guns," Jake said, shaking his head.

"Hmm," Claire said.

"Hmm," Jake replied.

"Okay, let's find something we agree on," Claire said. "Soft, hot, fresh-from-the-oven chocolate-chip cookies."

"I'm with you."

"Um, okay, Letterman over Leno."

"No question," Jake agreed.

"Cats over dogs?"

"No way. Dogs."

"Well, let me try again," Claire said, biting her lip in concentration. "Pepperoni, no anchovies."

"Now you're back on track."

"Classes where the teacher lectures instead of just assigning a lot of reading."

"Definitely. Mr. Gondin instead of Ms. Boyer."

"No contest," Claire agreed. "See, we're doing pretty—*ahh*!"

"Run for your life!" Jake shouted gleefully as the surf surged suddenly, foaming over Claire's feet.

"Boy, that's cold," Claire said. "I guess the tide must be coming in. What time is it?"

"Time for you to kiss me."

"Oh, you think so?"

"You don't?" Jake asked.

"I didn't say that," Claire said. She tilted back her head and let herself melt into his arms.

"*Ahhh, ah*, let's move up the beach," she said, breaking away suddenly as the freezing surf rose to cover her ankles and soak the hem of her jeans. "It's coming in fast."

They climbed the slope of the beach, retreating beyond the reach of the surf, and flopped down onto the sand in a low sheltered spot between two grassy hillocks.

"I have one," Jake said. "Beaches and surf over mountains and snow."

"That's a close one for me, but I think I can go along with you," Claire said. She nestled against his chest and gazed out across the water. Weymouth was over there, not exactly a metropolis, not exactly Boston or New York, but a city just the same. Full of people who typically did not know each other, people who could come or go at random, not on whatever schedule the ferry kept. "Do you ever stop to realize how unusual it is living on this island?" Claire asked.

"Well, there are only about three hundred of us, so I guess that makes us pretty rare," Jake agreed.

"I know there are other islands—Matinicus, Monhegan, all the ones down in Casco Bay, and so on—but even if you throw in places like Nantucket and Martha's Vineyard, I'll bet there aren't as many people living on islands in this country as there are people over in Weymouth."

"The few, the proud, the islanders," Jake said ironically.

"Do you ever wonder about when we go off to college how we're going to fit into a world where you don't already know everyone?"

"I have to admit I haven't really thought about it."

"Sometimes I'm jealous of those people," Claire said wistfully. "It must be nice to be anonymous. It leaves you free to be whatever you want to be. You can reinvent yourself. If you make a mistake or do something awful, who's going to even remember? Whereas here . . . here it's just hard ever to live down your past."

Jake cuddled her up under his chin. "I don't think you have anything to live down."

"Maybe you don't know everything about me," she said in a low voice.

"I've known you all your life."

"You didn't know that blue was my favorite color," she said, trying to sound lighthearted again.

"I know what's important," Jake said confidently. "And I like it this way. See, over there in Weymouth, or I guess anywhere in the rest of the world, you can never be sure who your friends are. People can hide their true selves."

Claire waited, listening to the surf crash once, twice. "You thought you knew Zoey," she said in a near whisper.

She could feel the sudden heavy thudding of Jake's heart, the way his breathing grew shallow. "Yeah. I did, didn't I? Well, I guess that's a good point. I guess even here you can never be totally sure who you can trust."

"No, you never can be sure," Claire said.

"It's a hard lesson to learn," Jake said. "It tore me up pretty good. It still does when I think about it. Not that I'm saying I miss Zoey or anything," he added quickly.

She scooted around halfway to face him, and they kissed.

"Don't you ever do that to me, okay?" Jake said in a half-pleading, half-joking voice. "Don't suddenly turn against me. I couldn't take it twice."

Claire was on the edge of reassuring him, of saying, *Of course not, Jake, of course I'll never betray you,* but something inside her choked off the words. She was already betraying him. "Kiss me again," she said.

When he had pulled away he smiled at her, his open, honest eyes glittering in the starlight and the ocean's phosphorescence. "Just always be straight with me, Claire. That's all I'll ever ask."

The words pained her, but the darkness hid her involuntary reaction. She couldn't bring herself to answer, to add a fresh lie on top of the old lies. Instead she distracted him again. "That's *all* you'll ever ask me?" she asked archly.

"Well —" He laughed.

She kissed him again. The serious mood was dispelled. His sad, hopeful pleas had gone unanswered. It was so easy to deceive Jake. It would have been so much harder with Benjamin. Benjamin would have instantly recognized her evasiveness and been on her like a cat on a mouse.

She pushed Jake away, feeling unsettled. It was fun, trying to manipulate Benjamin. Benjamin could take care of himself. Jake could not. She could lie to Jake forever. She could manipulate Jake as much as she wanted to. She already had.

"Is something the matter?" Jake asked.

"No," she answered shortly.

"Did I do something wrong?"

She'd had two major boyfriends in her life, boyfriends that amounted to anything—Lucas and Benjamin. Neither of them easily hurt. Neither of them exactly saints. Jake was different. Jake was . . . was waiting expectantly for her to say a kind word.

"No, Jake, you didn't do anything wrong," she said, a little wearily. "I doubt you've ever done anything really wrong."

Claire

Diary:

Not much weather today, a perfectly clear night, and they say the
high-pressure system may stay over
the area for a week. Good weather is
so boring. I need a storm.

Or maybe I'm just being cranky.
I feel agitated and unhappy. I should
feel great. I'm happy with Jake,
really. He's such a relief after
Benjamin.

Still, it's a big change. It's not
just like changing clothes. I have to
be different with him than I was with

Benjamin. If I ever insulted Jake
the way I sometimes did Benjamin, I
think Jake would really be hurt. It's
not that he doesn't have a sense of
humor, he does. He's funny in a
different way, though. Not as biting as
Benjamin was. Nicer.

Nice. Decent. Sweet. Straightforward.
Honest.

I like Jake a lot. I can't wait till
I can be with him again. And I know
he feels the same way about me. The
problem is each time we're together,
I feel like I'm tricking him somehow.
I feel like I'm outsmarting him. And
that just makes me mad, although I'm
not sure if I'm mad at myself for
being so manipulative or at him for

being so easy to manipulate.

I guess this is what it's like going out with a nice guy. No wonder Zoey finally dumped him. It's too much pressure to live up to. It's a strain being around someone who's nicer than you are.

But I can't be honest with him. I can't. He would never understand or accept the truth.

Honesty would just hurt him. So I have to go on deceiving Jake, to protect him, and of course he'll go on believing me.

I could really use a storm. A major blow, lightning, thunder, driving rain. That would shake me out of this funk.

Fifteen

Nina threw her pillow at the alarm clock the next morning, knocking it to the floor, where it kept right on blaring overly loud music. She climbed out of bed, reached for the clock, realized too late that her foot was caught in the sheet, and tumbled onto the floor, where she was at last able to turn off the radio. She glared up at her poster of the Red Hot Chili Peppers.

"Is this really the way to start out a day?"

Although, it was, at least, a Friday. Even the worst Friday was better than the best Monday.

She untangled herself from the sheet, put the clock back on her nightstand, and fumbled in her bulging purse for a Lucky Strike. Only two left. She popped one in her mouth. *You'd think they'd last longer when you never actually light them,* she thought.

Friday. Cool. It was possible to survive Fridays. Fridays could be handled. There was still school, but on Friday even the teachers just wanted to end it all. Teachers tended not to do tests on Friday because they didn't want to spend their weekends grading them.

Ah yes, Friday.

She padded out into the hallway and down to the bathroom. Ha! She had beat Claire to it. Excellent. Now, to waste as much time as humanly possible and pay her sister back for yesterday morning, when Claire had left her with about seven minutes and no hot water.

How long a shower would it take to use up all the hot water?

"Let's find out," Nina said gleefully, turning on the hot-water tap in the bath as she calmly brushed her teeth over the sink.

She looked at her reflection in the mirror, which was just beginning to steam up. "This is the day," she told herself, pointing her foamy toothbrush for emphasis. The direct approach. It worked for Aisha. Why shouldn't it work for her?

"Benjamin, I would like to go out with you. Yes, on a date."

What's the worst he could say? *I love you like a sister*? Ooh, that would hurt. How about, *Nina, I just don't think of you in that way*? Not to mention, *Go away, why would I want to go out with you, you gorgon, when I can have any girl in the school, ha ha ha ha!*

She brushed some more and spit. He wasn't going to say that. She had never heard Benjamin call anyone a gorgon. Besides, how would he know if she was?

"The direct approach," she told her now-steamy reflection. "But first a long, long shower."

Aisha closed her eyes and stuck her face under the jet of hot water, rinsing away the soap, then tilted her head down to rinse away the shampoo. Conditioner? Yes, the stuff that smelled like coconuts.

Would Christopher like that? What if he didn't like coconuts? A lot of people didn't. Maybe she should use the stuff that smelled "like spring." Everyone liked spring, though Aisha doubted anyone really knew what spring would smell like. Flowers? Rain? Birds hatching?

Who cared what Christopher liked? She wasn't going to be inviting him to smell her hair. Besides, maybe she'd use some of her mom's perfume.

Only the scent wouldn't last till the end of the day, when Christopher was going to pick her up. Which also meant that her coconut hair conditioner wouldn't smell by then, either.

Maybe she should bring some perfume with her. Some scent that would blend nicely with the cotton candy and hot dogs and pony poop at the carnival they were going to down in south Weymouth.

Or maybe she should just cancel the whole thing. It wasn't too late. Later it would be too late. Later, when they were coming back on the late ferry and he tried to get her to kiss him.

No kiss. She had decided on that. The purpose of this date was just to show that she was definitely *not* afraid to go out with him, because she, unlike Zoey, could deal with guys without losing her mind.

So no kiss.

Except maybe one small one. Just to be polite.

She twisted the faucet and slid back the glass shower door.

Claire's teeth chattered as she snatched the towel from the hook and wrapped it around herself. What did Nina do in the shower for twenty minutes? She hadn't even left any lukewarm water, let alone hot. Well, she was definitely going to straighten this out with Nina before cold weather came. She wasn't going to freeze to death every morning while Nina used up all the hot water daydreaming about new ways to annoy people.

She grabbed a second towel and wrapped it over her shoulders.

Great. Ten minutes to get ready.

Friday, she realized suddenly. It was Friday. Tomorrow was the day Lucas would be leaving.

"Stay away from Zoey today," she muttered. Zoey would be wandering around like a zombie, no doubt. Even worse than she'd been the last two days.

196

She pulled on her robe, sudden anger making her movements clumsy. Then she ran up the stairs to her room.

Not my fault, she told herself. It was just the way things had worked out.

She pulled off her robe, balled it up, and threw it into a corner.

I'll wear something white today, she thought, looking at the contents of her closet. *Something in a nice, innocent white.*

Zoey dressed with numb fingers, pulling up her shorts and zipping the fly, buttoning the front of her blouse. She had to look like she was going to school. And yet she wanted to look perfect for Lucas. This might be their last day together. She wanted him to have a good memory of her.

The tears started again, as they had so many times, but she wiped them away determinedly. He was not going to remember her with red, swollen eyes. She would use some Murine. Gets the red out.

Was this all right? she asked the image in her full-length mirror. She looked like she always did, like the girls in the Land's End catalog—wholesome.

Was that what she wanted him to remember? She made an ironic face. Well, she was wholesome. It was too late for her to suddenly transform herself into Sharon Stone or Madonna. Although maybe that was what Lucas would have liked.

He wanted to make love to her. Maybe she should. Wouldn't that do more than anything else to ensure that he never forgot her? And that someday he would come back to her?

She grimaced at herself. "Yeah, he can come back to meet Lucas junior."

Although he probably had condoms.

Condoms sometimes broke.

But how could she say no when they had so little time left together? And did she really want to say no? She was getting ready to skip school for the first time in her life. Maybe it was time for another first.

She looked thoughtfully at herself and unbuttoned the top button of her blouse, showing just the edge of her white lace bra.

Then she shook her head and buttoned it again and walked from the room.

Nina desperately craved another cigarette. She knew it was insane, she knew she couldn't really be addicted because it wasn't like she even smoked the stupid things, but still, she wished she had one.

The ferry was coming into Weymouth. In two minutes it would be docking. Then she probably wouldn't have any time alone with Benjamin all day. Which would mean her next opportunity would be on the ferry coming home.

But what if someone else offered to take him to the concert? Everyone knew Benjamin liked the strangest music. Anyone might ask him out between now and the end of the day.

She bit her thumbnail, watching him from under her lowered brows as he calmly sat, reading a Braille book.

"Okay," she said, squaring her shoulders.

"Okay, *now*," she repeated.

"Really. I mean it. Now."

Suddenly she was walking, swinging her arms wide in a wild parody of nonchalance that was completely lost on Benjamin but would make her look like DORK SUPREME to everyone else on the boat.

"Hi, Benjamin," she said in some other girl's voice.

"Hey, Nina. What's up?"

"I guess Zoey skipped school to hang out with Lucas, huh?"

"Looks that way," Benjamin agreed, nodding glumly.

"Well, there's a concert, you know. Like, um, Batch."

"Batch? You mean Bach?"

"Of course that's what I mean," she giggled, blushing furiously. Was that really how you pronounced it? "Can't you tell when I'm kidding?"

"Usually," Benjamin said, looking puzzled.

Too late to stop now. "So, Bach is playing down in Portland would you like to go because I could drive my dad's car and it would be kind of fun I mean I know you like that kind of music andsodoIreally."

"Huh."

Nina took a breath. "Of course if you don't—"

"Are you just doing this to be nice, because I would pay for the gas and all."

Nina froze. Was that a yes? Yes, yes. It was almost certainly a yes. "It starts at eight thirty. Tomorrow. At night."

"Cool. We can catch the five ten. Grab something to eat when we get down to Portland. My treat on the food, since you're probably going to be bored all night."

"I don't think I'll be bored," Nina said, feeling almost giddy with triumph.

Sixteen

"See, the thing you have to do is control your fire," Christopher said, squeezing the trigger briefly and sending half a dozen very loud rounds into the target. "Most guys think because it's a machine gun they should just blast away." He squeezed off a quick burst.

"You're not hitting the little red star," Aisha pointed out, peering closely at the target.

"I'm blasting a circle *around* the star, see, then it will fall out and I'll have the fabulous blue-and-white teddy bear that I've wanted my entire life." He fired again, forming a circle halfway around the red star. "One more burst." He squeezed.

"That's it, pal," the attendant said in a bored voice.

"That's it?" Christopher demanded. "I'm out of ammo?"

"What can I say?" the attendant said with a shrug.

Christopher put the gun back in its cradle and turned to Aisha. "What can I say?" he mimicked. "No teddy bear."

"Want some cotton candy?" Aisha asked, holding out her half-eaten cone.

"No, let's go on the Ravin' Rodent," Christopher said. He pulled a bunch of tickets out of his pocket. "We've barely touched the rides."

Aisha followed him somewhat reluctantly. Thrill rides had never exactly been her thing. "Just don't blame me if I hurl pink," she said.

The line was short so late in the season, with almost all the tourists gone home. Aisha threw away the last of the cotton candy and licked her fingers clean. Then they scrunched side by side into the narrow red car. Christopher put his arm around her shoulders to make more room.

"I heard some kids were killed here when one of the cars jumped off the track, flew through the air, and crashed into the Tilt-a-Whirl," Christopher said conversationally.

"Really?"

"No. I just thought I'd make the ride more exciting for you."

"Thanks. I appreciate that."

"No problem."

Aisha tested the bar that held them down. "They do inspect these things, though. I mean, experts look at them and make sure they're all right?"

Suddenly the car jerked forward and began the slow, clanking ascent to the top. The carnival came into view around them, a sea of swirling neon surrounded by darkness. Off-key music blared from the carousel, and somewhere a persistent bell was ringing.

"I love roller coasters," Christopher said. "Especially this part. The anticipation."

"These rails look so rickety. Hey, I think there's a bolt missing. Right there." Aisha pointed at a section of track that passed beneath them. "I'm serious."

"At the top you have that pause, that first look down at the drop, and you think, Wow, what am I doing here?" Christopher offered philosophically.

"What are we—*Ahhhhhhhh!*"

"Yes!"

"Uhuhuhuhuhuh."

"Ha, look out!"

"Oh! Okay, that's enou-uhuhuhuhuh."

"Yahh yow, that was great. Here comes the loop."

"The what? Oh. Oh. *Ahhhhhh!*"

"That was excellent. I never thought such a small coaster would be that much fun. Come on, stand up."

"Is it over?"

"It's over, and they would like us to leave now," Christopher said.

Aisha opened her eyes and glared at him reproachfully. "You're a sick person, Christopher."

"I love roller coasters. If we're going to be . . . whatever . . . you're going to have to learn to like roller coasters. My great goal in life is to go to Ohio."

"Ohio," Aisha said as she walked shakily down the ramp.

"Cedar Point, the Mecca of great roller coasters. Roller-coaster heaven." He had a faraway look, his eyes shining with wistful anticipation. "Cedar Point. We could drive down next summer. Get a room at the Holiday Inn, spend all our time riding the coasters." He paused to consider. "Well, maybe not *all* our time."

"It's good to have dreams," Aisha said sardonically. "Even if there's no chance they'll ever come true."

"What, you don't think I'll ever get to Ohio?" he asked innocently.

"I don't think you'll ever get me to a Holiday Inn," Aisha said.

"Don't be so sure. You know what an overachiever I am." He laughed easily. That was one of his more attractive character traits, Aisha thought. He had a sense of humor, even about himself.

"How about a nice, slow, gentle ride?" Christopher suggested.

"Okay. Give my heart a chance to stop pounding."

"Uh-huh, right," he said noncommittally. He gave two tickets to the ticket taker and led her down the roped pathway to a row of boats.

"Does this involve plummeting down a waterfall and getting wet?" Aisha asked suspiciously.

"No waterfall," Christopher said. "See? They don't even have a safety bar, so how bad can it be?"

They climbed down into the boat together and again Christopher put his arm around her, although this time there was plenty of room. Aisha considered shrugging him off, but they'd been having a good time together and it would seem rude. Besides, he'd been perfectly well behaved so far. And it was just a little chilly in her sleeveless shirt. She had tiny goose bumps up and down her arms.

The boat meandered along an artificial stream, then slid into a dark tunnel, lit only intermittently by dim bulbs revealing dusty tableaux of plaster pirates gloating over papier-mâché gold coins.

"Sort of a low-budget Pirates of the Caribbean," Aisha remarked.

"Yeah, this ain't exactly Disney World," Christopher agreed, laughing. "But it is slow and gentle."

"I like slow and gentle," Aisha said.

She felt Christopher's arm tighten slowly around her shoulders. *That's not quite what I meant*, she thought. But instead of speaking, she just swallowed and pointed at the next tableau. "That one's really lame."

Now Christopher was sitting closer, his leg pressed against hers, his arm sliding down her back to encompass her waist. His warm breath was on her neck.

The boat slid out of the circle of light, into a still-darker part of the tunnel. There was no light. No sound but the trickle of the water and the beating of Aisha's own heart.

Now was the time to say no. Now was the time to tell him she did not want to kiss him, because she didn't really care about him one way or the other, was not attracted to him, was not interested in anything serious, was not going to fall for him just because they were both black in a nearly all-white school.

His lips were close. They brushed her cheek, searching in the dark. Then missed again, brushing her chin.

What did she have to do, draw him a road map?

She found his jaw with her fingers and guided his lips to hers.

At that precise moment, a flashbulb went off.

Aisha jumped back, startled. The boat plowed through swinging doors and emerged in the neon glow of the carnival again.

"I think that ride was a little too short," Christopher said, his voice an octave lower than usual.

She looked away, feeling confused and annoyed. And frustrated. "It ended just at the right time. I should have told you, I don't kiss on the first date."

"You don't?" Christopher said, smirking as he helped her up onto solid ground.

"That wasn't like a real kiss," Aisha said. "Besides, it was so dark I didn't even know where you were."

"Uh-huh."

"You folks care to buy the souvenir photo?" the attendant asked, holding out a Polaroid. "Two dollars."

"No," Aisha said quickly.

"Absolutely," Christopher said, pulling two dollars from his pocket. He admired the photograph critically. "Huh. You say that wasn't a real kiss?"

Aisha snatched the Polaroid from his hand and clapped a hand over her mouth. Christopher snatched the photo back.

"Why don't you just admit it, Aisha? You like me. You wanted me to kiss you, I did, and you liked that, too. Why is that so hard for you to admit?"

Aisha glared at him, then down at the photograph in his hand. Then, despite her best efforts to stop herself, she grinned sheepishly. "Okay, I didn't hate it. But I'm still not going to Ohio to ride roller coasters."

Claire pushed the last of her pecan pie halfway across the white linen tablecloth. "That is so rich," she said.

Jake looked greedily at the dessert. He had already finished his own. "You're not going to eat that?"

"You eat it," Claire invited, smiling in amazement as the last two bites disappeared almost instantly.

"I'm a growing boy," Jake mumbled apologetically.

Claire sipped her coffee. "That was a pretty good meal," she said. "Not quite as good as Passmores', maybe, but good."

Jake raised an eyebrow. "I don't know when I'm going to feel right about going into Zoey's parents' restaurant again."

"Think they'll poison you?" Claire joked.

"I don't know; it just doesn't seem quite right, you know?"

Actually, she didn't. She wasn't doing anything wrong going out with Jake instead of Benjamin Passmore. And Jake wasn't doing anything wrong by going out with her and not Zoey Passmore. Claire's inclination might have been to make that point by having dinner at Passmores'.

"I understand," she said.

"No point rubbing people's noses in things," Jake said.

This, from the guy who had punched Lucas almost the first time he saw him back from jail? But then, Claire realized wearily, that was all a part of it—it was one thing in Jake's mind to go right up and start a fistfight, because that was straight-up-the-middle. Taking Claire on a date to Passmores' would seem sneaky to him.

"You realize this is our first real date?" Claire said, breaking away from her morose thoughts.

He gave a leering wink. "Does that mean I get my first kiss all over again?"

"Anytime," she said, leaning through the candlelight to let him kiss her. It was a brief kiss, but full of tenderness. Also full of self-consciousness as Claire realized that some other patrons were watching.

"Come on, let's get out of here," Jake said, his voice low. "I already told Mrs. Savageau to put it on my dad's tab. He owes me for some work I did at the marina."

"Jake, I was going to pay half," Claire complained. "Come on, let me help out."

"No way," he said. He stood up and came around the table to pull out her chair.

Claire sighed and led the way outside, pausing only to tell Mrs. Savageau that everything was wonderful. Outside the air was cool and clear, and they strolled arm in arm along the waterfront, wandering in the general direction of Claire's home. The ferry was just coming in, rounding the breakwater, and they used the excuse to stop and make out a little, leaning against the shadowed side of a wooden souvenir shack.

"That's the ten ten," Claire commented. "I

didn't realize it was so late."

"If you remember, we got a slightly late start," Jake pointed out. "Certain people weren't ready at seven sharp like certain people said they would be."

"Certain people had to make themselves look good," Claire said.

Jake stepped back and looked her up and down, then back up again. "Mmm. I take it back. Definitely worth the wait."

"Hey, look," Claire said, laughing as she pointed toward the bow of the ferry.

"Is that Aisha and Christopher?" Jake asked rhetorically. "I thought she didn't really like him."

"Has an interesting way of showing it, doesn't she?"

"It looks to me like they're getting along," Jake said dryly.

"Young love," Claire said.

"They aren't the only ones," Jake said, suddenly sounding serious. "I have totally lost it for you, Claire."

"Jake—"

"No, I mean it. I'm actually glad Zoey dumped me. I mean, if she hadn't, you and I might never have gotten together. I've known you all my life, and yet I feel like I'd never really known you until that evening when you came to my room when I was depressed over Zoey and—" He shook his head helplessly. "It's like you rescued me."

Claire felt her hands clenching and deliberately forced herself to relax. Damn. He was going to say it, and there was no way to stop him.

"I love you, Claire." He held up his hand. "You don't have to say anything back, I know it's kind of quick and all, but I know how I feel."

"Jake, how can you know how you feel?" she asked miserably.

"Because I know you," he said.

Damn it, she raged inwardly. *Why is he doing this to me?* "You . . . look, you don't know everything about me, Jake. You really don't. I'm not exactly perfect, I'm—"

He silenced her with a kiss. "You are exactly perfect for me."

Claire returned his kiss, going through all the familiar motions. But inside she was boiling, raging. Something was gnawing at her, infuriating her and at the same time drawing a blanket of unhappiness over her mind. It was a strange, unfamiliar, unpleasant feeling.

He pulled away and whispered, "You're the best, Claire, the best."

The feeling grew, and suddenly the name for it popped into Claire's consciousness. Guilt.

Oh, Claire thought dismally as Jake held her tight to his chest, *so that's what guilt feels like.*

Seventeen

Zoey had spent the day with Lucas, walking the beach, climbing the winding paths up the ridge, strolling along Pond Road. They'd covered nearly every square foot of the northern half of the island.

Lucas was saying good-bye, again, to his home.

They talked of everything under the sun, of his plans and hers, their hopes and dreams. He talked about his mother, how sorry he felt for her, a shadow in her own home. And he talked about his father, how he admired him, despite everything, for his moral code, his ability to work without complaining, even his determination.

And Zoey talked about her own family, the way she felt her parents had never really grown up, the way they both felt somehow guilty because Benjamin had lost his sight. But the more she talked, the differences became so clear. Yes, her father still had one foot in the past, still played Grateful Dead records and wore a ponytail. And yes, her mother flirted too much with the guys who came into the restaurant's bar, and was, by her own admission, not into 'all that parental stuff.' But what was so clear was that in her family she was loved. And despite her parents' almost daily arguments, they loved each other passionately.

She had so little to complain of, really, and Lucas had so much. Without her, Lucas was utterly alone.

They had cried, and kissed, and hugged each other till it hurt. But they had not found a way to put off the deadline that seemed now to be racing toward them at a terrible speed.

They vowed to spend every last minute they could together. They also vowed they would never give up, that they would find a way to be together.

They said good night easily at midnight, knowing that it was only a rehearsal.

Zoey went through all the motions of going to bed, lying awake in her bed until she heard her parents come home from closing the restaurant and go to sleep. At two thirty she dressed silently, stole down the stairs, and crept out the back door.

The moon was still in the sky, turning the dew that had settled in her backyard silver. She made her way up the path. She saw Lucas in his window, waiting. He held up his hand and disappeared. Seconds later the front door opened silently and she flew into his arms.

They walked at a snail's pace up the stairs and into Lucas's room.

"I knew you'd come," he whispered.

"Of course. Nothing could stop me."

They kissed passionately, hopelessly, lying on his bed, a tangled mess of arms and legs and twisted sheets.

Zoey knew he wanted to make love to her. And she didn't know how she could refuse. In five hours they would have to catch the ferry. In nine hours he would be on a plane. In less than eleven hours she would be back on the island, alone.

Alone.

He lay on his back, she lay on him, looking down at his dark face, knowing that her tears were falling to mingle with his. Sadness swept them both up, dampening the passion that had threatened to carry them away.

They lay together in each other's arms, saying nothing. After a while Zoey felt she might even be sleeping, as dream images floated through her mind. Images of them together, happy in sunshine.

She even smiled, the first time in so long, as she constructed fantasies of how they could find each other again. Then her bleary, swollen eyes focused on the blue numbers of his clock. Four o'clock. Their time together had shortened by another hour and a half.

She stirred, and her lips found his in the darkness. Her fingers unbuttoned his shirt. He seemed to have stopped breathing, and then, his fingers, nervous, fumbled at the front of her blouse.

"You don't have to do this," he whispered.

"I know," she whispered back. Was she? Was she really going to do this? Or was this just another part of her fantasy of happiness?

There was a heavy clumping on the steps and Lucas froze.

"My dad. He's going to work."

"At four in the morning?" Zoey asked.

"Lobstermen start early," Lucas said.

They heard the sound of the front door closing and footsteps crunching on the gravel driveway. He had not bothered to say good-bye to his own son, Zoey realized. And with Mr. Cabral gone, any last hope for a reprieve was gone, too.

Suddenly a voice came from the front yard. Not Mr. Cabral's deep, accented voice. They hesitated only a split second, then they raced to the dormered window, both half-dressed.

The sky was still dark and the moon had set, but the porch light showed them clearly—Mr. Cabral, standing, smoking a cigarette.

And Claire.

Zoey looked at Lucas questioningly and saw the trace of a smile on his lips.

"I'll be damned," he said softly.

They dressed quickly and went down the stairs, no longer caring what anyone thought, and emerged as Mr. Cabral was walking away.

Claire had her back to them. "Mr. Cabral," she

called out. "You have to do it. You know it's the right thing."

For what seemed an eternity, Mr. Cabral stood, his cigarette burning away in his mouth, staring down toward the distant dock. At last he half turned, looking over his shoulder at his son. "Lucas," he said, giving the name an odd pronunciation. "Lucas, you better stay."

For a moment it looked as if he might have something more to add, but then, grinding the butt of his cigarette out underfoot, he set off again, rounding the corner and disappearing down Center Street.

Claire turned to face them, her mouth set in a grim line. "I suppose you're wondering what I'm doing here at four in the morning," she said, her attempt at humor falling flat.

"What *are* you doing here?" Zoey asked.

Claire ignored her, focusing on Lucas. "Look, Lucas, there's something you have to understand. I really didn't remember. After the accident I really did not remember."

Lucas nodded and remained silent.

Claire drew in a deep, shaky breath. "I just remembered a week ago. Things just started coming together. Mostly I guess because you returned. I guess it jarred my memory. Anyway, I've known since then. I didn't speak up because of my dad . . ."

Lucas nodded again. "I understand."

216

"I don't," Zoey said.

Claire looked surprised. "You didn't tell her?"

Lucas made a dismissive noise. "One thing you learn right away in jail—everyone in there claims to be innocent. What was the point in one more convict running around claiming he got screwed?"

"Innocent?" Zoey said, trying to piece together some understanding.

"Lucas wasn't driving the car the night Wade McRoyan was killed," Claire said wearily. "I was."

Zoey rocked back on her heels and put a hand over her heart. "You?"

"No one knew the truth but Lucas and my father," Claire said. "Not even me. Lucas took the rap because . . . well, we were good friends."

"I loved you," Lucas said simply.

"And then my father got into the act. He helped Mr. Cabral out with a loan he needed to keep his boat. He wanted to make sure Lucas wouldn't change his mind and recant. Especially after everyone realized they were actually going to send Lucas to jail." Claire took another deep breath. "My father knows I know," she said. "I told him I'd keep it quiet. He says people might think he'd broken the law himself. The loan to your father might look like he was paying you to confess."

"I'm not going to tell anyone about that part of it," Lucas said.

Claire sagged in relief, but Zoey was outraged. "Why would you protect Claire's father?"

"I wouldn't," Lucas said. "I'd protect my dad, though. He doesn't know why Mr. Geiger arranged that loan. I know my old man's a bastard, but he would never sell me out for money, and it would tear him apart if he knew the whole truth. From here on out the story will just be that I was a dumb kid, so madly in love that I confessed to protect Claire. That's ninety percent of the truth, anyway."

Claire nodded. "That's a better percentage than we've had around here lately."

"Have you told Jake yet?" Lucas asked.

Claire hung her head and answered in a whisper. "That's next."

"Poor Jake," Lucas said sincerely.

"Yeah," Claire said. She looked at each of them, her dark-in-dark eyes almost lifeless. She tried out a smile that quivered and collapsed.

"You say you've remembered for a week, at least," Zoey said. "But you kept it a secret till now. What made you change your mind?"

This time Claire did manage a soft, sad smile. She sighed deeply. "I don't think Lucas ever had any illusions about me being perfect, back when we were together. And I know Benjamin didn't. But Jake . . . Jake thinks I'm like him. He thinks I'm sweet and honest and fundamentally decent. The more he trusted me, the worse I felt. The more he accepted my de-

218

ception, the more I couldn't stand myself."

"You felt guilty," Zoey said.

"Yeah. It took me a while, but then I realized that was it." She made a sour face. "Nasty feeling. I'm going to have to learn how to get over it." She turned away and took several steps before calling over her shoulder, "You two can get back to *whatever* it was you were doing."

Lucas grinned and took Zoey in his arms. "Can we?"

Zoey gave him a quick peck on the cheek, then firmly pushed him away. "I'm very, very sleepy. I think I'll head on home."

"Will I see you tomorrow? I mean, later today?" Lucas called after her.

"Yes," Zoey said, twirling around in sheer happiness. "Actually, you will."

She tapped at the sliding glass door for a long time. The sun was just beginning to peek over the horizon, a faint glow that threw the ridge into relief, black against a pearl gray sky. Claire was exhausted. She hadn't slept at all this night.

She had tossed and turned in her bed, arguing one side and then the other. Concern for her father, fear of losing Jake, versus the sense that either way she would lose Jake. How could she ever really pretend to love someone when their entire relationship was built on deception?

And as much as she tried to dismiss it, the

image of Zoey crying, having to say good-bye to Lucas, and even the image of Lucas, whom she had once loved, suffering yet again for a crime he didn't commit, kept coming back.

She tapped again at Jake's door. Sooner or later he would wake up. It wasn't even five yet, a ridiculous hour for a visit. But Claire was determined to get it all over with. She couldn't let Jake learn the truth secondhand. She had to tell him herself.

A memory popped to the surface of her mind. Benjamin, of course, just a few days earlier . . . had it really been only a few days? It seemed like forever. He'd pointed his sunglasses at her and said, "In the end, as self-serving and ruthless as you are, Claire, when the line is drawn between right and wrong, I think you'll do the right thing."

The memory brought a smile. Benjamin would feel so smug, being proved right.

The door slid open quite suddenly. Jake stood there blinking sleepily, wearing only a pair of boxer shorts. "Claire?"

"I'm afraid so," she said.

"Is something the matter?" Then his face brightened as he thought of another possibility. "Or are you just here to—"

"I have to talk to you," she said. "Can I come in?"

"Of course." He was fully awake now and obviously puzzled.

She entered the dark room. He offered to turn

on the light, but she said no, the darkness was fine. They sat together on the edge of his bed.

"What's up?" he asked.

She took his hand in hers. Then she leaned over and kissed him, not a passionate kiss. Closer to a farewell.

"I don't know any easy way to say this," Claire said. "For a long time I didn't remember the details of the night Wade died."

She felt him stiffen, but she maintained her grip on his hand. "But now I do remember. We had all been drinking. Lucas and I and Wade. All of us."

"I know you were all drunk," Jake said. "But only Lucas was driving drunk."

Claire felt a tear trickle down her cheek. Damn. She didn't want to do that, but she was just so tired. "Lucas wasn't driving," she said.

For a moment Jake froze. Then, slowly, he pulled his hand away.

"Lucas was in the backseat," Claire said. "In fact, he was saying we should pull over and walk home. But I wouldn't listen."

"You?" he whispered.

"I was the one driving the car, Jake. And the more Lucas complained, the more I would swerve around, making a big joke of it. Until that last split second when I realized we were going to hit." She took a deep, shaky breath and forged ahead. "And just so the whole truth is out, once

221

and for all, I saw the tree, and I knew we would hit it. And at the very last second I yanked the wheel over so that it wouldn't hit my side of the car. I saved myself. And I killed Wade."

Eighteen

Nina was up earlier than she had ever been on a Saturday, managing to catch the usual seven-forty ferry to Weymouth. The night before, just as her father was heading to bed and was yawning and vulnerable, she had talked him out of his American Express card and half the cash he had in his wallet.

She hadn't gone on a date since . . . well, for a very long time, and she needed clothes, a purse, shoes other than boots, all the usual date stuff. Probably stockings. Lip gloss, eyeliner, breath mints.

Obviously, Benjamin wouldn't really know how she looked, but still, she didn't want to show up and have him look great and her look like crap. What if someone he knew was there and came over and said, Hi, Benjamin, how come you're going out with a girl who's dressed like a skank?

It was pretty bad if you couldn't manage to dress better than a guy who couldn't even see himself in a mirror.

Once off the ferry, she caught the bus out to the mall, arriving just as the doors opened. Instantly she felt overwhelmed. If only she had Zoey with her. But today was the day Zoey would be saying good-bye to Lucas. Not a good day to ask her along on a shopping trip.

Naturally, she felt sorry for Zoey, but Nina's presence would not be welcome while Zoey and Lucas said their sad farewells. And as for Aisha, Nina didn't really want to try to convince Aisha to get up this early on a Saturday.

Too bad Claire wasn't the type of sister she could really share this kind of an experience with.

Plus, of course, it was Claire's former boyfriend she was going out with.

"Okay," she said, standing uncertainly at the mall's crossroads, "all you need is one complete outfit. Sophisticated, but not like you're making a big deal out of it. Attractive but not sleazy. Conservative enough for classical music and yet with a style all your own."

She set off like an explorer through uncharted wilderness. She had shopped at the mall, of course, but usually only in certain areas. She'd never even been inside some of the shops. Possibly because she had never consciously bought anything *for* a date. Which, she supposed, did make her a little backward compared to most junior-class girls.

"Face it," she muttered, "you're a little backward compared to most sixth-grade girls."

She didn't know why she hadn't dated very often, or why she had never dated any guy more than twice. Usually her dates amounted to meeting casually at a movie, or a quick stopoff at a burger place. She'd only ever kissed one guy and that had grossed her out.

The truth was, most guys grossed her out.

Except Benjamin. He was so different. She knew he would never be disgusting, the way guys often were. He would always treat her with respect, and that was important. Unlike when she had gone out with George O'Brien and he had kissed her and then tried to touch her breasts.

The memory made her heart race, and she realized her palms were sweaty. She had totally panicked when George had done that. So utterly uncool of her. George had gone around telling everyone she was a lesbian. Which she wasn't. In fact, she had more experience than people knew. More than Zoey and probably Aisha.

That memory made her even more uncomfortable. She beelined for a bench and sat down beside an old man. She fumbled a cigarette out of her purse and stuck it in her mouth.

"You're not going to smoke that, are you?" the old man asked.

"Actually, no," she said. She took several deep

breaths and wiped her hands on her shirt front.

Why were these things out of her past suddenly reemerging? She hadn't thought about all that in a long time. At least not outside of the dreams she sometimes still had. Was it because she was finally going out with Benjamin? Was that it?

But Benjamin wasn't George O'Brien.

And Benjamin wasn't her uncle, either.

She looked at her fingers and saw they were shaking. She sucked deeply on the unlit cigarette. *That's all in the past, Nina,* she told herself. *Years and years ago. Over and done and forgotten. Things happen, and then you go on.*

What if Benjamin tried to kiss her and the panic happened? Like it had with George? Was that why she had gagged in the movie theater when Benjamin had leaned close? Was she still capable of losing it the way she had with George?

She'd rather die than act that way with Benjamin. How would she ever be able to face him again?

But that wasn't going to happen, she reassured herself. This was Benjamin. Gentle, smart, funny Benjamin. Her friend. Her trusted friend.

And besides, he couldn't do anything she didn't want him to do. After all, he was blind, and that did give her a certain advantage she had never had back . . . back then.

"All right, shake it off, kid," she challenged

herself. The old man turned and stared. "Sorry, sir, I was just talking to the voices in my head. They want me to shoot Michael Bolton, but I'm refusing."

The old man gave her a startled stare that had the effect of instantly putting her back in a better mood.

She pulled out her father's American Express card and looked at it. "All right, let's you and me do some damage."

Nina arrived at Benjamin and Zoey's house at four forty-five, wearing a black dress, black pumps with heels that made her wobble and lurch, real stockings that itched her thighs, a silver necklace and bracelet, and enough perfume to fumigate a barn. She felt like the largest, most conspicuous dweeb on earth.

Zoey's reaction when she opened the door was not promising. "Nina? What are you . . . Nina? Is that a dress? And hose? Did someone die?"

Nina gave her a dirty look. "Didn't Benjamin tell you? We're going out to hear Bach. You know, Bach, I'm sure? Naturally I mean Johann *Sebastian* Bach, who lived from 1685 to 1750 and is considered the leading composer of the late baroque period."

Zoey stared at her. "Is this one of those cases of demonic possession? Have you been worshipping Satan again?"

Nina brushed past her into the entryway. "So tell me the truth, is it too much? It is, isn't it?"

"That's not it, it's just that—"

"Damn," Lucas said, nodding appreciatively at her. "Little Nina is suddenly all grown up." He grabbed her around the waist and swung her in a graceful circle.

"Lucas? What are you doing here? I thought today was the day you were, you know."

"Didn't Claire tell you?" Zoey asked.

"I haven't seen Claire all day," Nina said. "I've been buying clothes and memorizing fun facts about old Johann Sebastian. Tell me what?"

Zoey exchanged a look with Lucas. "Claire should probably tell you," she said.

"I would browbeat you into telling me," Nina said, "but my thighs itch, and I'm really here to pick up Benjamin. Is he ready? We have to make the five ten, and I'm not fast in these shoes."

"I'll go get him," Zoey volunteered.

"So, what do you really think," Nina asked Lucas, holding out her arms to give him the full effect. "You're a guy and all."

"That's very observant of you, Nina," Lucas said, giving her a wink. "What do I think, as a guy? I'll tell you what I think." He grabbed her around the waist. "Quick! Before Zoey gets back! Let's do it, right here on the floor!"

Nina felt a tremor of fear before she realized that Lucas was obviously kidding. She pushed

228

him away. "I guess that's a compliment. Kind of."

"You're a babe," Lucas said sincerely. "What are you going to do? Pick up guys down in Portland whenever Ben's out of earshot?"

"No," she said, blushing a little.

"Well, it's probably a good thing Benjamin can't see you tonight," Lucas said. "He might start thinking of you in a whole new way."

Nina rolled her eyes in exasperation. Obviously Lucas didn't get it.

Benjamin arrived with Zoey a few steps behind. He was dressed in a suit and loosely knotted tie. He took a quick turn as he came in. "Sorry to keep you waiting, but Zoey told me you were showing leg tonight. I thought I'd better go beyond my usual concert attire of jeans and a jacket and go all out and wear my dead-relative clothes. How do you like the jacket? I hear it's plaid."

Nina grinned. The suit was black, like most of what Benjamin owned, because black was an easy color to match. "I think the plaid jacket clashes just a little with the striped pants."

"How does Nina look?" Benjamin asked.

"She looks sophisticated and—"

"No, not you, Zoey," Benjamin interrupted. "What do you know? You're a girl. Lucas?"

"She looks too good for you," Lucas said. "I give her a thumbs-up. Way up."

"You're both sexist scum," Zoey said disgustedly.

"We better get going," Benjamin said.

"Yeah," Nina agreed. "I wouldn't want to miss anything. You all know how I love baroque music."

"Oh, right," Zoey said. "You just won't shut up about baroque music."

"This is very sweet of you to give up your Saturday night for me," Benjamin said.

Nina blushed again and muttered a quick good night to Zoey and Lucas. She took Benjamin's arm, and they crossed the yard together.

"You don't have to guide me," Benjamin said. "You know I have this island down like the back of my hand."

"Oh, yeah, I did know that," Nina said awkwardly, releasing her grip. Then she saw something that made her stomach churn. "It's Claire!"

Her sister was coming up the street looking angry, or at least distracted.

Nina slapped her hands down to her side and sidled away from Benjamin. She hadn't exactly mentioned to Claire that she was going out with her recently ex-boyfriend.

Claire caught sight of them and came rushing up. "Has either of you two seen Jake at all today?"

Nina shook her head violently, still expecting Claire to lash out with some choice bit of sarcasm.

"I haven't," Benjamin said.

"Okay. Okay. Damn. Um, is Zoey in?"

"She and Lucas are both inside," Benjamin said.

"I'll go ask them," Claire said, immediately heading for the house.

"What was that all about?" Nina asked as she urged Benjamin down the road.

"I'm not sure," Benjamin said in a troubled voice.

"I can't believe she didn't give me a hard time," Nina said.

"Why would she?"

Nina shrugged. "You know. Because, you know, you were her boyfriend and all. And we're, you know . . ."

"Mmm," he said, still frowning in a preoccupied way. "It's not like she'd be jealous. I mean, it's just you and me."

Nina stopped and glared at his back as he walked on. *It's not like she'd be jealous*, she mimicked silently. *It's just you and me.* She looked down at her expensive, painstakingly chosen outfit, with her tight, uncomfortable shoes. All this, and he still didn't get it. All this effort and he still thought of her as his little buddy. Damn him to hell and back again. The insensitive toad.

"Come on, Nina," he called over his shoulder.

"I'm coming," she muttered through clenched teeth.

"Well, walk up here with me," he said crankily. "I can't talk to you when you're dragging back there. Besides, I want to make everyone who sees us jealous."

"Why would they be jealous?" she subtly mimicked his own tone.

He shrugged. "Everyone's jealous of a guy with a beautiful girl on his arm."

Nina sighed. Okay, maybe he wasn't a complete toad.

Nineteen

Claire spilled out her fear to Zoey and Lucas. She had told Jake the truth early that morning. Jake had said very little, just turned his back on her, and when she had tried to put her arms around him, he had told her to leave.

Later that afternoon she had tried to call him, but there had been no answer.

She had gone over to his house. His yellow pickup was gone, and when Claire peered through the sliding glass door into his room, she had seen a pile of empty beer cans shoved half under his bed.

She had looked for him everywhere, called everywhere, but no one had seen him. She was worried. He was probably drunk, and in his truck, somewhere on the island.

"I don't know where to look that I haven't looked," she said, sitting stiffly on the chair in Zoey's room. "There's only one place . . . And I don't want to go there alone."

Lucas caught Zoey's eye. "We'll go with you," Zoey said.

The three of them piled into the Passmores' island car, a wreck even by island standards. Zoey drove along South Street to Coast Road. There was no question in anyone's mind where they should look.

At the end of Coast Road where the asphalt gave way to gravel and sand, where a huge tree still bore the scar of a deadly impact, they spotted the pickup truck parked in the ditch.

Jake was slumped over the wheel, unmoving.

Claire leapt from the car and ran, followed closely by Zoey and Lucas. She threw open the door, her heart pounding, her mind swimming in fear.

She saw Jake's breathing and, putting her hand to his cheek, felt the warmth. She nearly collapsed with relief.

"He's all right," she said. "Just passed out."

"Thank God," Zoey whispered.

Lucas gently pushed Jake back onto the seat and raised his legs into a prone position. Then, with a glance at Claire, he removed the keys from the ignition and handed them to her.

"I'll wait here with him," Claire said. "Till he wakes up."